UNPREPARED

D. A. RAMSEY

AND

JIM RUSH

A DAYDREAMER BOOKS PRESENTATION

DAYDREAMER BOOKS

Cover design by: 314 Creative, 4469 Iroquois Trail
Duluth, GA 30096
www.314creative.com

Layout by: SelfPublishing.com, 51 East 42nd Street, Suite 1202
New York, NY 10017

Web Site by: INS Digital Media
www.insWebsites.com

International Standard Book Number (ISBN)
Paper: 978-0-9787110-5-4

Standard address Number
SAN851-4186

Printed in the United States of America

1st Printing

Acknowledgment

I am forever grateful to the wonderful people who have inspired and encouraged me along my journey in life and in my Healthcare and Public Health career.

Special thanks to Ray Brown, Jim Machart, Joe Cappiello, General Mike Wyrick and Tom Runyon. I owe so much to the late Joe Langer for being the most loyal and wonderful friend a person could hope for.

Thanks to Dr. Dani Babb for her encouragement and her support of my Disaster Readiness work.

A special thanks to my wife Vivian for believing in me and my potential to contribute to the body of knowledge in Disaster Readiness.

Thanks to Debbie Ramsey for her writing skill and her perseverance in making *UNPREPARED* a reality.

UNPREPARED

"He went forth conquering, and to conquer."
—Revelation 6.2

"Say: Surely my prayer and my sacrifice
and my life and my death are (all) for Allah,
the Lord of the worlds."
—Quran 6.162"

PART I

Moscow
Spring 1998

A plane circled over the Dubai airport. Anatoly Buskeyev looked out the window of the 747 jet liner and thought about the events that had led him, and his wife Irena, to this end. He wondered if his decision had been the correct one. Glancing at Irena's face, he knew that, deep down in her heart, she wanted this. He also wondered if he wanted it as much as she. Now, thinking about the implications of his act, he wasn't sure of his own mind. Had this been the right move?

In the solitude of the first class cabin, he let his brain go into overdrive, questioning his motives. He vividly recalled the day when Abu al Mussari approached him as he stood, waiting in line outside the grocery store, for supplies and a few potatoes. Times were tough. The motherland was undergoing change. Revolution was on the lips of every radical in the country. However, for Anatoly and Irena, things would be very different. Change was imminent.

Anatoly had been the Deputy Director of Russia's Nuclear Storage and Maintenance Command facility, a very high level government post. And although the responsibility was immense, the pay had become meager. With the country undergoing reconstruction, teetering on the edge of collapse, the government had little money to pay anyone, and there had been times when Anatoly didn't receive any monthly compensation. Consequently, they barely made enough to get by. He tried to tell himself that things would change. That life would get easier when things became more "democratic".

As for Irena, she was a scientist working on the very technology it was his responsibility to guard. In his mind, he was defending Irena. By ensuring the safety of the nuclear arsenal, he was protecting her, as well as his countrymen.

Irena was the lead scientist in a group of nuclear engineers using miniaturization techniques that had been developed in the United States. With the new miniaturization method, a ten kiloton weapon could be enclosed in a much smaller package. Thus, transporting one bomb would be much easier. Not only could a smaller, lighter aircraft be used, but moving the weapon on the ground wouldn't require the massive trucks as in the past. The weapon could be stored in a crate and then moved about in a medium sized moving van.

In the early years of their life together, the Buskeyevs had money. Compared to their average comrade, and as trusted agents of the nation, they had lived a life of relative ease. They had a comfortable apartment in an upscale section of Moscow. They also had each other. Anatoly believed that life had a purpose. However, he was also a pragmatist. As the Soviet Union started to crumble around them, money had become scarce. Anatoly feared for his, and more importantly, Irena's safety.

For two long years the couple scraped by. Most of the family heirlooms had been sold for little more than a pittance, just to be able to buy the bare necessities, and those had to be obtained from the black market. Thoughts of defecting had crossed Anatoly's mind, and he even had discussions with Irena about that as an option. He knew, with their backgrounds, they could go anywhere in the world. However, she was resolute. Born and educated in the Soviet Union, it was there she would stay. Things would get better she had said. Life was all about balance and things had a way of correcting themselves. But Anatoly knew Irena's heart. She was becoming embittered. Things weren't getting better, and she felt that Russia had abandoned them.

Near the end, they had lived like paupers in a run-down converted hotel. And, for Anatoly, the ultimate humiliation was sharing a lavatory with other tenants. A bath had become a luxury as there was rarely any hot water. Heating oil outages had become commonplace and their main staple had become potatoes. Meat was out of the question as it had become much too expensive for their tight budget. Irena had started to lose weight, so much weight that Anatoly had become concerned about her health.

Then, one day, Abu al Mussari, a man with political talent, natural charm and the gift of persuasion had come into their lives, and nothing had been the same since.

Moscow
Fall 1997

Hezbollah intelligence agents had identified a target. The information had been transmitted to the headquarters in Tehran for approval. A Hezbollah Intelligence Officer, Asim Kassam was living quite comfortably in Russia on money supplied by Hezbollah. His main goal was to find a scientist willing to aide the Iranian government in carrying out their holy plan.

Kassam had been watching Nikolai Popov, someone whom he believed to be ripe for the picking. Nikolai worked as a safety inspector in the same nuclear storage facility as Anatoly Buskeyev. This gave Nikolai the ability to come and go from the compound without raising eyebrows. Unfortunately, Nikolai had suffered a mental breakdown due to the recent hardships endured by many of the Russian scientists. In a deeply depressed state, and before Asim could approach him with the divine plan, Popov had taken his own life.

In the meantime, the Buskeyevs had become more visible, as well as very interesting, to Kassam, so he trained his sights on the pair. Information on the couple had been gathered and sent back to Tehran. Over the subsequent weeks, the Islamic Clerics reviewed the data that had been pouring in. It was determined that someone with better skills than Asim Kassam was needed for this enlistment. Once the choice had been agreed upon by all the ruling members, and the decision made, Abu al Mussari was sent to Russia to do the recruiting.

And Mussari was good at his job. He had a way of persuading

people to do a certain thing, even if it went against everything they believed in. His approach was simple and direct. He had an air of confidence and a belief in "self" that transcended anyone who came before him.

In the early days of his adult life, Abu al Mussari proved to be a ruthless, cold-blooded killer. He had slit the throat of an acquaintance. As the man lay dying, gasping for air and choking on his own blood, Mussari thought nothing of cleaning the blade of his knife upon the man's blood-soaked shirt. His only offense being that he disagreed with Mussari.

On another occasion, Mussari killed the eldest son of a man, Gahlib Safar, who neglected to show up on time for a meeting. Mussari arrived at Gahlib's house, and once inside, found a birthday celebration under way. He casually strolled over to a young boy, and speaking to him kindly learned that it was his party. Mussari then grabbed the boy and, in front of the rest of the family, shot him in the head. Amidst the screams of the women, and obvious distress of Gahlib, Mussari demanded that they leave immediately, saying they were holding up an important meeting. Later that night, when they returned to Gahlib's home, Mussari threatened to kill the remaining members of the family should his name be mentioned in the murder of the young Safar.

When Mussari was recruited by members of Hezbollah, he quickly proved himself to be a trusted member of the inner circle and they taught him patience and diabolical deviousness, although killing was never far from his mind.

A Hezbollah chieftain, a man Mussari regarded highly, had been known to declare, "You have been touched by the hand of Allah." Those words, more than anything, were the driving force in Mussari's life. He truly believed that he had been touched.

Everything was stored in Mussari's memory. He never kept notes of any kind. If he was ever to be found out, there would be no paper trail indicting him in any act of malfeasance. To say his memory was photographic would be an understatement. Not only could he recall conversations word-for-word, but he could also "see" things that had been written down. Another generous gift from the benevolent Allah.

Over the weeks, Mussari waited and watched as Anatoly came and went from his lowly apartment. He followed every move Anatoly and Irena Buskeyev made. In time he learned that Anatoly was a victim of habit and never deviated from his daily routine. That one fact made his job easy. So, armed with that knowledge, Mussari decided to move the timeframe forward in which to make his approach.

The day was sunny and unusually cold. It was Tuesday and Anatoly regularly stopped at the store to pick up a loaf of bread. Today, the line was longer than normal, and that boded well for Mussari.

Warming his hands by blowing into them, Anatoly shifted his weight from foot to foot as he stood in the slow-moving line. He was chilled to the bone and his mood was sinking as rapidly as the pale Russian sun. He was not looking forward to telling Irena that another day would go by without heat. There was barely enough fuel remaining to cook with. They would have to rely on layered clothes, blankets, and each other for warmth again on this night. When he pulled himself out of his reverie, his eyes met those of a man he had never seen before.

"Good evening, comrade. My name is Abu al Mussari," the

man said with a warm smile. His outstretched hand bore an expensive kidskin glove.

Looking up and then down at Mussari's clothes, Anatoly couldn't help but notice that they were not threadbare nor were they out of style.

With a handshake in response, Anatoly introduced himself, and then said, "What, may I ask, are you doing in a bread line? You don't look to me to be in need of a hand-out."

"I am here to meet you, comrade," Mussari said with a twinkle in his eyes, and an affable, sideways grin. "Come with me. I would like to have a conversation, and this is not the place for our discussion."

Anatoly responded, cynically, "I would like to speak with you, sir, but it will have to be later. As you can see, I am waiting for my crust of bread."

Abu al Mussari chose his words carefully, and with another warm, genuine smile, said, "My friend, I can supply you with bread, and potatoes, and meat, and vodka, and anything else you might desire. All you need do is name it. Please, come with me. I think what I have to say will be of some interest to you."

• • •

Abu al Mussari asked for a few minutes of Anatoly's time, nothing more. Anatoly obliged. What did he have to lose? The men started to walk slowly down the street in the direction of Anatoly's apartment.

"Comrade Buskeyev, I come to you today as a trusted friend, a friend of the Soviet Union and a friend of Anatoly

Buskeyev. Tell me, how long have you been working for the state?"

With a look of surprise, Anatoly responded, "How did you know that I work for the state?"

"I am not a fool comrade. I didn't happen to just pick you off of the street. I watch, I learn."

Nodding as if he understood, Anatoly responded honestly without giving a second thought to his new acquaintance or the information he was about to divulge. Feeling completely at ease with his new companion, he said, "I have worked in the weapons program all of my adult life. I received a Ph.D. in Nuclear Physics over twenty-five years ago."

Mussari listened intently knowing that the information Anatoly was providing matched the intelligence he had received. So far, so good. Anatoly was not trying to pretend to be something he was not.

"I am proud of the work I do," Anatoly stated bluntly as he drove his hands down deeper into his tattered jacket pockets. "My job is very important, but I'm afraid that the nuclear program will soon be dismantled. I don't know where I will go or what I shall do if that happens."

"You believe these rumors?" Mussari asked innocently.

"Yes, of course."

Appearing to be intrigued, Mussari asked, "Why?"

"Money problems at the highest levels of the government, that's why. They can scarcely pay me now, and things are not getting better, comrade."

The men walked along for a few blocks in silence. Just as Anatoly was ready to make the turn to go down his street, Mussari stopped him.

"Walk with me down this road. I have something of interest to show you."

"I must get home. My wife will have a meal prepared and I don't want for our dinner to be ruined, and without our weekly handout, she would be doubly angry," Anatoly replied, not wanting to keep Irena waiting.

"This will not take too much of your time, I assure you," Mussari said, trying to convince his companion.

"Perhaps I can meet you in an hour and bring Irena with me," Anatoly offered as an alternative.

"Please, comrade, we are here now," Mussari implored, convincingly. "When you see what I have to show you, you will then understand why I have brought you here." After a slight hesitation he added, "I will make it worth your while."

Looking over his shoulder, in the direction of home, and then into the seemingly kind eyes of his new friend, Anatoly relented.

The things Mussari had promised earlier were too much to resist.

Irena carefully placed a spoon and a knife next to the two bowls on the table. She nodded in acceptance and then paced the little room as she waited for her husband to arrive. The soup had been turned off and the lid placed securely on the pot to keep the heat from escaping. There was very little fuel left in the cook stove and she was conserving as best she could. Her hope was that Anatoly would bring fuel home tonight along with the rationed bread and potatoes for the next few day's meals. If he was unable to get the cooking fuel, and she knew that was a possibility, the last little bit in the stove would be just enough for tea with their morning toast. After that, it was anybody's guess when more would come available or where it would come from. Yes, times were tough, but they were Russian and could stand up against any hardships. She looked at the clock. Anatoly would be home in minutes. She continued to pace, but more than anything, it was to help keep warm.

As she wandered around the tiny apartment, thoughts she had tried to stifle started to hammer at the back of her head. Miserable life, she thought. "What happened to the days of prosperity? The days when Anatoly and I could make a good living in our motherland? The days when Russia was a world power and one to be reckoned with?" she asked the empty room.

Irena continued to walk, her hands balled up into little fists, shoved down in the frayed pockets of a sweater that belonged to Anatoly. She looked at the meager furnishings, and the threadbare rugs. Sitting down in one of the mismatched chairs of the dining room set that had seen better days, her thoughts ran wild like a startled deer through the wood. Even a teenager in the United States of America would never consider living in such squalor, she thought.

"How has it come to this?" she questioned and then looked at the clock. She was becoming concerned over Anatoly's tardiness.

The men had walked several short blocks, and then rounded another corner. The road was nothing more than a very narrow alleyway. Anatoly thought he would have missed it had he been walking on his own. Mussari stopped in front of a weathered door with a square peephole barred against prying eyes. He knocked three times, waited for a few seconds and then rapped again three more times. A voice from within called out something in a language not unfamiliar to Anatoly. Mussari answered in the same foreign language. The slider on the peephole opened and the voice on the other side grumbled an unintelligible response and the door opened.

The men entered a poorly lit corridor and walked a few feet. Abu al Mussari turned to his companion, and said, "My friend, you are about to see something few men will have the honor of witnessing."

Mussari opened another door and the bright lights flooded the hallway. The men entered the illuminated, noisy, room. Anatoly was overwhelmed by the size of the area and the number of people inside. There he stood, in a very large gymnasium, with several boxing rings set up inside. Each ring held a pair of contestants. The men were decked out in full boxing gear, and were surrounded by trainers, coaches and handlers. Anatoly's eyes opened wide in appreciation.

Watching his companion with keen awareness, Mussari never let down his guard or let his demeanor change in any way. With a smug nod in the direction of the action, he said, "I can see by your expression that you are a fan of boxing. What man isn't?" he added rather nonchalantly.

He led Anatoly ringside where the conditioning specialists were tending to the athletes. Mussari introduced Anatoly to another man, one Anatoly noticed had been watching them with some interest.

The new man's name was Gregor Vishkin, a stout gray-haired Russian. After a brief introduction, Gregor took Anatoly on a tour around the vast gym. Anatoly watched as men sparred in the rings. They bobbed and weaved as they tried to outwit their opponent. Others were hitting heavy bags which were hung from the ceiling, while still others were jumping rope and performing other types of aerobic exercise.

"These men are dedicated to the sport," Gregor said as they walked slowly around the gym. He continued his commentary as he swept the area with the wave of his arm. "Everyone here dreams the same dream. Each man desires to, one day, fight for the title."

The pair continued their slow march around the perimeter, watching the various activities taking place. The slapping of skin, and men grunting in exertion, echoed in every corner of the huge room. The smell of perspiration and musty towels filled Anatoly's nostrils, yet he couldn't take his eyes off of the men in the rings.

"Unbelievable, the amount of pain one man's body can endure, don't you agree?" Mussari asked as they finished their trip around the gym.

With a bold look and eyes narrowed, Anatoly responded firmly, "Yes, I have to admit, that is the case." Then, pounding his chest he added, "But, I am Russian. I, too, know what it is to live a life of pain, and suffering. Not physical, such as these boxers endure, perhaps, but pain nonetheless."

"And that is precisely why I have sought you out, my friend. For now, I will let you go home to dinner and your wife. You see? I told you this would not take up too much of your time," Mussari countered.

"Why did you seek me out?" Anatoly questioned.

"Wait here. I won't be a moment," Mussari said, deliberately ignoring the query. He turned and walked rapidly to the back of the gym, rounded a corner, and disappeared. He returned moments later with a package tucked securely under his arm. "I sought you out because you are Russian. You work for the state and you deserve better than this," Mussari said, pointing to Anatoly's attire. With pride Mussari continued, "Look at me. I made the decision to become involved in art of pugilism."

When it was evident that Anatoly wasn't catching on, Mussari tried to explain. "Before Russia's government fractured, boxing was sponsored by the state, was it not?"

Knowing that fact to be true, Anatoly grunted in agreement.

"Today, boxing is a business, just like any other business. We have sponsors that provide money … lots of money … because it takes a lot to get an operation this size from amateur ranks to the next level: professional. We have men fighting all over, in places like Chechnya, Uzbekistan and Kazakhstan. But, more to the point, they're winning," Mussari affirmed, proudly. "Soon, we will be taking our champions to Germany, and the U.S., to fight against some of the most famous names in the game."

Anatoly knew, as the world recognized, that Russian boxers were not just good, they were magnificent. It seemed like an age ago, but he remembered watching the Olympic Games on television and cheering on his team as they beat the rival U.S. boxers at their own game. A slight smile crossed Anatoly's lips, one that Mussari did not miss.

Holding out his hand in fellowship, Mussari said, "Why don't you meet me here tomorrow night? Bring your wife if you'd like, and we can talk more. Here, take this."

"What's this?" Anatoly asked. He took the parcel as he shook hands with his new friend.

"Give it to your wife. It is a very small token of my appreciation for taking you from your dinner table tonight. There is enough meat and ample fuel for you to enjoy a delicious dinner this evening," Mussari said with a glint in his eyes.

Not knowing how to react, and not wanting to reject such a thoughtful gift, Anatoly nodded hesitantly. "I will be here tomorrow night, at this very time," he said.

Walking the short distance home, Anatoly wondered how such a place could exist less than a stones throw from his apartment, and he not know about it. Opening the door, he was met with a chilly reception. He walked past Irena and sat down at the table. The package from Mussari was hidden beneath his jacket. The concern she had earlier had been replaced by anger. Anatoly hadn't noticed that she was perturbed which only infuriated her more.

Watching him pass, and with arms crossed tightly across her chest, Irena stated curtly, "At the very least, can you give me a reason why you're late and caused our dinner to be ruined?"

"Hmmm? Oh, I am sorry for being late, but I met the most interesting character while standing in line at the grocery," Anatoly replied as he looked her in the eye.

Irena's anger flared anew with Anatoly's apparent disregard for her current emotional state. "Where are the things you were supposed to pick up? Were you able to get more fuel? I had to use the last of what we had to reheat your dinner. Now, we have nothing for the morning," she scolded.

Sheepishly, Anatoly said, "No, I'm afraid I didn't stay in line. I went with the man I met. He had something he wanted to show me."

"You left the line to go see something a stranger wanted to show you?" Irena asked, incredulous. "I'm beginning to think you're losing your mind, Anatoly. What could someone that you've never seen before possibly have that is so enticing that you had to leave the line, and ignore our plight at home?"

Irena was talking to him like a child and it was beginning to grate on his nerves. To keep from getting annoyed himself, Anatoly spoke slowly and succinctly. "Yes, I left the line. The man I met tonight obviously has money. I could tell by his clothes, and by the way he carried himself, that this was a man of means. He spoke very good Russian, even though he is clearly not. He appears to be of Arabic descent."

Realizing she had become shrill and condescending, Irena tempered her tone. "This made you ignore your task? Ignore me? I've been so worried," she replied, quickly picking up on the fact that Anatoly's newfound friend had money.

"No, my dear wife, I would never ignore you." And then, with a twinkle in his eye, he said, "It was what he offered that piqued my interest."

Reaching into his jacket, Anatoly removed the package and placed it on the table.

Sitting together they ate their dinner of fresh ground beef, slices of French bread and potatoes, while Anatoly discussed, in great detail, the conversation he had had with Abu al Mussari. Irena listened with rapt attention.

Irena was ready to get back to the life they had once known. It was not a life of excess, but they certainly lived better than most. They had a comfortable home in an affluent section of Moscow where they interacted with other talented and intellectual people from all walks of life. After all, they had devoted their lives to Russia. They had even given up the family she knew Anatoly had wanted, so they could dedicate all their time to their work without distraction. However, it didn't matter to Irena. She had been content to serve her country in any manner they had asked of her. How dare Russia abandon them now?

Mussari strode confidently into the gym. There was an intent look on his face as he continued to watch the boxers going through their routines. He had a good feeling about his initial contact with Anatoly Buskeyev. His first report to the Imam will be a good one. While he was going over the details of their next meeting in his mind, Fayed Mohamed, one of the men standing with Gregor, approached with questions. He was one of two trainers. Both were Hezbollah and assigned to a boxer.

Speaking in Farsi, their native tongue, Fayed quizzed his superior. "Do you think Anatoly will be prepared to join our jihad to free the world of infidels and their decadence?"

"Yes, I believe he will ... eventually. He is coming here again tomorrow night. I told him to bring his wife, at which point, I will treat them to a very nice, and very expensive, dinner. I can be quite persuasive."

"Yes, of that I am fully aware," Fayed remarked with the frankness of one who knows.

"You are also aware that I taught Asim this very same approach, of using food to persuade? Nikolai was weak. He buckled under the pressure. That is why we take precautions and exercise patience when looking for the right man. I can tell that Anatoly will not break, but he will bend. We have reached our objective. Now, all that is left is to persuade," Mussari stated confidently. He concluded their conversation by saying, "It's getting late. If I am to entertain the Buskeyevs tomorrow evening, I had better be prepared. Only the finest of food, wines and vodka will do. I have a few stops to make on my way home this night."

"You seem confident that he will be here," Fayed responded.

"Of course, how could he not?" came the glib reply.

• • •

The day went by slowly for Anatoly. Thoughts of the coming meeting with his new acquaintance rolled uncontrollably through his head. Scenarios of how he could possibly fit in with the group played in his mind. However, the obvious reason never occurred to him.

When the clock finally chimed the end of his shift, Anatoly rushed home. He and Irena cleaned up and donned their finest clothes. They each had an outfit they considered to be decent enough for the outing that night. Irena was an attractive, statuesque brunette with striking gray eyes. "The eyes of a cat," Anatoly had told her on the day they met, and that's all it took. Her intelligence was only outmatched by her outgoing nature and charm. Irena was immediately hooked on the muscular, handsome man with wavy black hair and mustache. But Irena had noticed his eyes as well. They were clear blue, intense, and deeply set beneath prominent brows. "The face of a thinker," she had told him. She had been mesmerized by his eyes and after years of marriage, still found Anatoly to be the most handsome man she had ever met.

Before they left the house, Irena asked, "Do you think I look presentable?"

"What sort of question is that?" Anatoly asked in astonishment, his eyebrows arched in surprise. Irena was not one to question how she looked.

In direct response, she stated, "I don't wish to look foolish and ruin your meeting."

"Don't be silly, my dear. You look lovely," Anatoly reassured her. "When did you ever look foolish? Besides, these men are not interested in what you are wearing."

Irena figured that to be a true statement, but it only left another question in her mind. Just what were those men interested in?

The Buskeyevs walked the few blocks to the gym. When they reached the alleyway, Irena slowed nearly to a stop and gave Anatoly a questioning look. He just cupped her elbow in his hand and led her down the narrow road until they reached the door. Just before Anatoly knocked, the door opened and Abu Al Mussari appeared, wearing a smile of greeting. "My friend," he said with obvious delight.

Anatoly shook hands with Mussari, and took the opportunity to introduce Irena. While the trio exchanged pleasantries, a brand new, black, Mercedes Benz limousine pulled up at the end of the alleyway. It stopped and waited. With a sweep of his hand, Mussari led the couple to the car. A chauffeur emerged, opened the door, and the companions sat comfortably inside.

As the car drove down the street, Mussari asked, "Would anyone like a glass of wine?"

Trying to maintain an easy outward appearance, a very nervous Irena answered casually, "Yes, that would be nice, thank you."

It was difficult for her not to stare at Mussari. She was intrigued by him. Not wanting to appear rude, she concentrated on looking out of the window at the scenery passing by.

"You seem distracted, comrade Buskeyeva," Mussari stated as he handed her a crystalline glass filled with expensive brut champagne. "Please, rest assured, there is nothing to fear. Tonight, you will learn many fascinating things, over an exquisite meal, I might add."

The limousine left the confines of the city and traveled a few miles into the country. It was dark by the time they reached Abu Al Mussari's house, but the Buskeyevs could immediately see that his home was nothing short of palatial.

The chauffeur helped Irena out of the car. Anatoly took her arm in the crook of his, and they followed Mussari into the foyer which was lit by the most extravagant crystalline chandelier Irena had ever seen. Beauty surrounded them. Everywhere Irena looked her eyes fell upon very expensive furnishings, paintings and marble sculptures.

Helping Irena out of her coat, Mussari handed it to the maid who immediately disappeared into another room taking Irena's coat with her. Mussari then led the couple to an elaborately furnished drawing room where he offered refreshment. He said, pleasantly, "Please, make yourself comfortable. My home is yours."

Irena still felt out of place in the ornate surroundings. It hadn't been that long since they had fallen into poverty, but their new acquaintance had made if feel as though it had been a lifetime ago. With slight, watchful hesitation, Irena took mental notes of everything in the hopes of uncovering some hidden agenda. But she wondered, if she were to find one, would she utter a sound?

While Abu Al Mussari was preparing martinis, Anatoly took his wife's hand and gave it a little squeeze, as if to say, "This is it. We have arrived." Irena squeezed his hand in return and then placed both of her hands in her lap. She didn't want to give anything away to her host. A little half smile of victory graced her lips.

Mussari had positioned himself in the room so that he could see every movement his guests made. Even though his back was to them, the mirror above the bar was set at a convenient angle. As he set about mixing the drinks, he watched as the couple passed their quiet signals to each other. He laughed inwardly knowing the words he spoke to Fayed were true. They were hooked.

Handing each of his guests a martini, Abu al Mussari sat on an ornate chair facing them. Getting comfortable he asked them how they enjoyed their dinner the previous night.

With a coy smile, Irena said, "The meal was lovely, thank you. The cooking fuel was very timely, too. I don't know when we will be able to repay your kindness."

"No payment is necessary. The pleasure was all mine. You see, I understand your predicament. For many years you were held in high esteem within your government. Now, they treat you like an unwanted guest. For the time being, they tolerate you, but only because they need you."

Nodding in agreement, Anatoly added with conviction, "That is a true statement. Once the program is dismantled, we will be tossed out in the street like a cur without so much as a second look. All the years of commitment and dedication, ignored."

"For many years you have protected your people. You should be treated as heroes, not pariah. I had learned of you and your wife from a colleague, and thought, 'These are people who would understand a good opportunity when they see it.' That is why I approached you on the street."

Before Anatoly could question further, the call to dinner

came and they moved from the drawing room to the formal dining room. The table was made of oak and massive in its scope. The meal consisted of prime rib and more side dishes than the Buskeyevs could count. They ate until they could not swallow another bite. They sat at the table while the after-dinner drink was served and then moved to another room. This was a cozy library and a warming fire was glowing in the hearth.

The small talk finally turned to boxing. Mussari offered Anatoly a humidor packed with a variety of cigars, and said, "What did you think of our little enterprise?"

Pausing for a moment, and puffing happily on the end of an expensive, hand-rolled Cuban cigar, Anatoly said with a light laugh, "I wouldn't exactly call that a 'little enterprise' comrade."

"Ah, certainly, that it is not. I'm sure you are wondering what you could possibly do for us.

"I will admit, the thought had crossed my mind," Anatoly responded, completely at ease.

"You obviously have no money for investment, and your background is not in the pugilistic arts; although, I am sure you know much about the sport," Mussari countered.

"Yes, I am a fan, but have not had time recently to keep up as I would have liked," Anatoly explained.

"Translator," was Mussari's one word reply.

Acting as though the answer resided on the tip of her tongue, Irena blurted out a response. "Translator. Yes, of course. Anatoly speaks several foreign languages."

"I told your husband yesterday, we are preparing our team to take on the German and American boxing federations. Not the amateur ranks, mind you, but the professionals.

Unfortunately, most of our boxers speak only Russian. We are in desperate need of translators if we are to be successful in our travels abroad."

Looking at her husband with adoring eyes, Irena said with pride, "Anatoly speaks seven local languages, as well as English and German. He would be indispensable."

Directing his next question to Irena, and knowing the answer, Mussari asked, "You speak English and German as well, am I correct?"

Not finding the question to be out of the ordinary, Anatoly replied with a smile. "Yes, of course she does."

Letting the clock tick away a few minutes before continuing, Mussari let the Buskeyevs digest the conversation before asking, "What do you think? Is this something that would be of interest to you? Naturally, we would pay you handsomely for your services, Anatoly. The bonus would be that you, and your wife, would get to do some traveling, see some of the world."

"That is a very generous offer, comrade, but you do understand that Irena and I must discuss this in private before I can give you an answer."

Anatoly's demeanor was very businesslike. Even though his immediate reaction was to jump on the offer without hesitation, it warranted serious discussion. He figured Irena would want him to take the job, but he didn't want to appear desperate or overanxious. The words he spoke were true. He wanted to talk it through with Irena first.

"Of course," Mussari responded, aware that Anatoly was going to accept the offer, and that this was merely a stall tactic meant to make him sweat a little bit. One thing he could never understand, though, was why some men, in cultures different from his own, deferred to their wives instead of making sound decisions based upon the facts presented. But, he didn't want to drive the Buskeyevs away, so he just agreed with them … for now.

"It's getting late and Irena and I must be up in the early hours for work," Anatoly stated as he slowly arose from his resting place on the comfortable sofa.

"How rude of me, of course. Let me have the car brought around to take you home."

Mussari left them and called the butler to prepare the Buskeyevs for their return trip home. A few moments later a servant appeared, but the coat she gave Irena was not the same one she had arrived with. This was a full length mink coat with a matching hat. Anatoly was prepared to refuse the gift, but Irena allowed Mussari to help her into it.

With eyes alight, Mussari asked, "A wonderful surprise, is it not?"

"I'm afraid that I'm speechless," Irena said as her hand stroked the pelt lovingly.

"It is a gift. Please, accept it as such and don't give it a second thought. As you can see, I can well afford such luxuries."

The men shook hands and Mussari kissed Irena's cheek. The Buskeyevs took their place in the back of the limousine as it headed in the direction of the city, taking them to their modest home.

Anatoly watched as Irena continued stroking the fur. "It is not a living thing, Irena. It no longer breathes life, so why do you pet it as if it were a purring cat?"

"Oh, but you are so wrong, Anatoly. It does breathe life. It has breathed a new beginning into ours," Irena stated confidently. This was a woman who knew what she wanted, and of this Anatoly had no doubts.

The Buskeyevs spoke little on their ride home, as they each considered Mussari's offer. Anatoly's thoughts centered on the world of boxing and the exciting places he would be able to take Irena in their travels.

Irena thought about money and status.

Neither one knew exactly what was in store for them.

Sitting behind his desk, Abu al Mussari turned on the television to watch the news. He also read the daily papers, to keep on top of other operatives carrying out their missions in other parts of the world. He then read the mail to keep abreast of events at home. He knew that, since its founding in the 1980s, Hezbollah's mission had been the elimination of America's world influence. This was particularly evident in the Middle East, where Islam's archenemy, Israel, has been enjoying the protection of the United States. He had to smile as he recalled reading a recent article which had described Hezbollah as "The A Team" of terrorist groups. Not knowing exactly what that meant, Mussari did his homework. Doing some in-depth investigation, he had to admit, Hezbollah's operatives matched Hollywood's depiction of men who could plan, organize, direct and control its members throughout America, and the world.

Hezbollah wanted to be fully capable of causing catastrophic damage to America's financial, manufacturing and healthcare sectors. The damage inflicted upon the American society would have to be so devastating that it would be impossible for them to defend Israel in any meaningful way. With one swift blow, Hezbollah would be in the position of not only eliminating America as a world power, but annihilating the State of Israel and the Jews as well.

Mussari knew how to achieve that objective, and there was only one thing left to do in attaining that mighty goal against the "Great Satan" and its puppet state. That's where Mussari came in. It was his divine duty to recruit Anatoly Buskeyev.

He placed a call to Qusay Sharaf, in Dubai, to begin putting the wheels in motion.

. . .

Several days had passed without a word from Mussari, and Anatoly was beginning to wonder if he had imagined the entire affair. But, then he would see Irena strutting about in her mink coat and he knew it was not a dream. Secretly, he hoped things at home, in Russia, would settle down a little before making such an important decision. Something didn't feel right about the entire matter, but he couldn't put his finger on what it could be.

Walking to his apartment from the train station, Anatoly bumped into Abu al Mussari. With a friendly handshake, Mussari said, "How are you, comrade?"

Exhaling a slow breath, Anatoly said, "I am fine, although a bit tired from the day and ready for the evening." Anatoly left it at that, wondering if Mussari could read his thoughts. After all, the man had a habit of materializing out of nowhere, like a wizard.

"Have you had an opportunity to discuss the situation with your wife? I know this is a big step and a serious decision. After all, you hold a very high position within your government."

"Yes, but one that will not be worth much before long, as you well know," Anatoly responded as he started in the direction of home.

Walking along, Mussari asked, "So, can I take from your answer that you have decided to take the position I have offered? Or, perhaps you still need time to think it over?" He knew Anatoly had to be ready to bite.

"You made a generous offer. How can I refuse?" Anatoly stated matter-of-factly.

"Wonderful," Mussari exclaimed, and his gloved hands came together in a muffled clap.

"But I have to admit, I'm not comfortable with this idea of traveling at this particular moment. There is so much uncertainty in the world, so much unrest."

Caught off guard by Anatoly's response, Mussari needed to come up with an enticement that would close the deal once and for all, particularly for Anatoly. His gut feeling was that Irena was not the one harboring doubts. Thinking fast, he said, "Right now, plans are in the making, to go to Germany. As you know, we have an exhibition match there. Why don't you come along with us? It will give you an opportunity to realize exactly how you will fit in, and also how much we need your services. You will then see, first hand, how well we will be received in other countries. There is nothing to fear. We would be leaving in just over two weeks."

"Let me think about it. I will have to discuss it with Irena and don't know if she would want me to go," Anatoly replied honestly.

With a casual shrug, Mussari said, "Bring Irena along. She's more than welcome to join us." With a wink, he added, "Besides, I believe she could use a vacation."

The men parted company and Anatoly walked the rest of the way home with Mussari's offer utmost on his mind. He knew Irena would be delighted were he to take the position, but he had a niggling feeling scratching at his brain, one he couldn't shake, nor could he explain.

When he entered the cramped apartment, he took off his hat and coat, and went in search of Irena. He found her, sitting comfortably, reading the evening news. Setting the paper down, she listened attentively as Anatoly recounted his conversation with Mussari.

When he finished the story, he said, "I find it strange that he always knows where to find me, and when."

"Why would he not?" Then using his nickname, she said, "He's waiting for you to give him an answer, Tolya." Just as curious as Mussari to Anatoly's intentions, Irena questioned, "What are you going to do?"

"What do you think I should do? I'm very confused about this whole thing," Anatoly said as he walked into the small kitchen to put a kettle on for tea.

Irena countered, "I see no harm in going to Germany." When Anatoly looked at her with a blank stare, she added, "Do you?"

"I suppose not." Anatoly reacted to the whistle of the teapot and brewed two cups. Handing one to Irena, he said, "I will have to make arrangements at work to have someone cover for me. I can always tell them that there is an illness in the family."

Hoping to prod him along, Irena responded in a positive manner. "Germany is a lovely country. We have always wanted to go there. I suggest taking comrade Mussari up on his offer. Then, you will know for sure, once and for all, if you will want to take that position."

Letting out a long sigh, Anatoly said, "It will do us both some good to get away, even if for a little while. And you are right. This trip could reveal many things."

Anatoly sat quietly sipping on his tea, his mind wandering. He thought of many things, but his thoughts did not stay for long on any one thing in particular, while Irena could think of nothing but regaining their social status and improving their rank.

The following week went by without a word from Mussari. Each day Anatoly expected to see him appear somewhere, but there was never a sign of the man. Then, on Monday morning, while on his way to work, and just when Anatoly least expected it, Mussari's car appeared seemingly from nowhere. It pulled up beside Anatoly as he walked to the train station.

The darkened window slid silently down, disappearing into the recess of the door, revealing Mussari's smiling face. "Good morning," Mussari exclaimed as he took in a breath of cool morning air. "Nothing like a brisk walk to get the blood moving, don't you agree?"

"Yes, good morning," Anatoly answered, trying not to sound surprised, but his face betrayed him.

Noticing the look Mussari felt vindicated. He said, "I'm sorry I have not been in contact with you these past many days, but as you probably know, I have been very busy getting the team ready for the trip to Germany. I took the liberty of making reservations for you and your wife. I hope I was correct in my assessment of your ultimate decision."

"Yes, that is good news. Irena will be very excited. It has been her dream to visit Germany. Our career path didn't lend itself to travel abroad, and holidays were always spent close to home." After a slight pause, Anatoly added, "Actually, it's been quite a while since we have been able to take any meaningful holiday."

Still smiling, and nodding in agreement, Mussari countered, "Then, I am pleased to be able to provide this reprieve for you. It will only be for a few days, but you will have a wonderful time. I guarantee it."

Anatoly looked over the top of the car, into the distance,

clearly mulling something over in his mind. Astutely, Mussari didn't miss it. "Can I assume that you are troubled over leaving your work for a few days?"

With another stunned look, Anatoly responded, "Why yes, that is what was of some concern to me. It is that, and the fact that Irena and I have security clearances at the highest levels. It will take time to get the visas in order."

"Well, comrade, I believe I have just the answer for you. I took the liberty of having one of my contacts at the Russian Federal Security Service start the process of getting your Visas submitted and secured. I have been assured that they will be ready in time, so that is no longer a problem."

"Very good," Anatoly responded, but a question came to mind about how Mussari would know someone of such authority in the Federal Security Service. Then, the thought quickly evaporated as he realized that money not only bought power, but influence as well.

Quick to deflect any further questioning, Mussari continued, "I thought it prudent to start the process. Since Frankfurt is the city we were going to visit, I thought it would be a nice gesture to provide something of interest to Irena. I happen to know a very prominent professor by name of Heinz Geisler. He has invited you both to visit his Science Institute.

"That was very thoughtful," Anatoly replied, but his look was wary.

"I hope that you do not view any of this as being too forward. I knew we would need every available minute to get you on the plane. I firmly believe that you will be very pleased once you see how smoothly this operation runs." Not wanting to lose his quarry, and knowing he needed to change the tenor of the conversation, Mussari added, "Even if you decide not to join my organization, you and Irena will have a wonderful time. You have my personal guarantee. Come, let me give you a ride. It seems to be colder than normal out this morning, and that coat of yours is not going to keep the chill away. I will take you to the store to purchase one befitting this weather."

Suddenly, self-conscious of his appearance, Anatoly declined the offer. "I have but a few blocks to go to catch my train. Besides, I must make sure I have someone in place to cover my desk while I am away, and that means an extra stop. I do not wish to delay you and your plans for the day. By the way, when will we be leaving? I must know in order to make firm arrangements."

"Of course. We will be leaving very soon, Wednesday morning to be precise. If you could see your way clear of taking the rest of the week off, I will make sure that you and Irena have the wardrobe necessary for the meetings and dinners which have been scheduled while we are away. This is a business trip after all."

Before the men parted company, they agreed that someone from Mussari's organization would come by the next morning to escort Anatoly and Irena to the store for a day of shopping. Apologizing, Mussari said that he would not be able to join them, and insisted that they not concern themselves over the price tags. He viewed it as an investment in the future of Russian boxing. He then invited the Buskeyevs to dinner to celebrate their first day of freedom from their life of depravity. Mussari insisted they wear attire that suited a formal affair. Again, a limo would be there to get them. He made of point of telling them to have their luggage packed. The intention was to dine with the entire group that would be going to Germany. Everyone attending would stay at the same hotel and then leave together in the morning. The men would be spending many days together, in close confines, within a strange city. Knowing how skeptical Anatoly had been, it was Mussari's objective to make him feel as comfortable as possible.

When Anatoly turned to go, Mussari had his driver wait. He knew Anatoly was still harboring doubts. A master of reading body language, he wanted to watch Anatoly's. He gave a smug grin as Anatoly walked away with the stride of a self-assured man, his head held high. When Anatoly didn't turn to look, Mussari knew that he was slowly winning his confidence.

He sat back in his seat, and with a wave of his hand, Abu al Mussari's chauffeur drove to the gym.

Late Tuesday afternoon, the limo appeared right on schedule. Wearing their newly acquired wardrobe, Irena and Anatoly stepped from the confinement of their dismal surroundings into a world of bright lights and overindulgence.

When they reached their destination, Mussari met them at the curb, and then helped Irena from the car. Leading the way, he said, "Come with me and I will announce your arrival. Everyone here is very excited. Not only is a Russian going to be working with us, but one of great stature and renown."

Not knowing that he was being played, Anatoly swelled with pride. He was soon to be recognized, and appreciated by his own people, for the work that not only he, but his wife, had done for their county throughout the years. This was a glorious day.

Once the introductions had been made, the group dispersed. They mingled, munched on caviar and hors d'oeuvres while waiters brought an endless supply of the finest wines, champagne and expensive liqueurs. Irena felt right at home.

With good humor, Anatoly watched his wife through soft eyes as she laughed and glided among the other guests in her form-fitting evening gown.

The last few years had taken a toll on both their lives, but tonight Irena looked young and vibrant. Anatoly had nearly forgotten just how beautiful she was, and he found her to be the most attractive of the all the women in the room. He also had to admit, it felt good to be back in the world of money and influence.

Soon, everyone was seated. The table was set in white linen. Only the finest in expensive china, crystal and silver would be good enough for Mussari's guests. Salad, soup and bread were placed at each seat, and the festive group made small talk as they began their dinner. Mussari let a few minutes pass so everyone could get comfortable. Before they started their dinner, Mussari stood and tapped a spoon against a goblet to get everyone's attention. He had an announcement to make.

Speaking in a loud, firm voice, and in an animated fashion, Mussari began. "Good evening my distinguished guests. This is a great night for all who are gathered at this table, for we are here at a time when historic events are taking place. We have the good fortune to be a part of what I like to call 'a new Russia.' It is a time when the Soviet Union of old is in the process of transition. A transition to what, you may ask? The answer is one word, but it holds much promise. That word is capitalism. I can see puzzled looks as you wonder, what does this means to me? It means that, not only the State Boxing Program, but more importantly, the banks are now privatized. Make no mistake, this is no small thing." Mussari stopped for just a moment to let the last statement sink in. Watching the faces of his guests, he could see the questions forming behind their eyes.

Mussari continued with another question. "What has capitalism done for us? It has enticed very wealthy men from the International Boxing Federation, as well as other investors from around the world, to put money into my program. As you are well aware, Russian boxers are the finest in the world, bar none! And as such, they are deserving of monetary accolade. This week, we will show the rest of the world just what is in store for them when we present the first of our champions in exhibition."

Mussari looked around the table at the faces watching him. He had everyone's rapt attention. He then looked squarely at Anatoly and concluded his speech. With his glass raised in tribute, he said, "There are a privileged few who are a part of this 'new Russia'. That, my friend, is you and me."

Taking his seat, Mussari picked up his knife and fork and began eating. His speech created quite a stir at the table as people took up candid conversations, with capitalism as one of the main topics.

Irena couldn't help but smile as she nudged Anatoly. Leaning over to whisper in his ear, she said, "You are a Tzar among men at this table tonight."

Anatoly nodded, but with Irena's statement came that gnawing feeling of disquiet. Wanting to put it to the back of his mind, Anatoly joined an ongoing discussion about boxing, leaving Irena to fend for herself.

• • •

The next morning, at the appointed hour, everyone congregated in the lobby of the hotel. There were several vans, packed with equipment and luggage, while the entourage rode comfortably in limousines. The tiny caravan traveled without fanfare to the airstrip where they were ushered aboard a private jet. Mussari had decided to hire a charter service. The plush surroundings and personalized treatment was just one of the tactics employed by Mussari to help close the deal on all of his prospects.

The flight took less than four hours, but to Anatoly, it seemed to go by in a flash. The party atmosphere had continued from the previous night. Conversations were lively and there was ample food and drink. Everyone was in high spirits as they drank heavily; everyone except for the athletes. They were on a strict training regimen which alcohol was not a part.

The group arrived at their destination and the rooms were ready. The Buskeyevs were shown to a suite that was larger than their Moscow apartment. Everything about the hotel was five star quality. Taking it all in stride, Irena didn't seem to notice the disparity between the hotel and home. She didn't want to give the impression that she was unfamiliar, or uncomfortable in any way, with this lifestyle. Anatoly watched as she put their clothes away, happily humming a mindless tune as she moved lightly around the room.

"Aren't you thrilled to be a part of this, Tolya?" Irena asked as she placed his new shirts on a hanger to ease the wrinkles out of them. "To me, it is all very exciting."

Lazing comfortably on the king-sized bed, his arms behind his head, Anatoly replied, "Yes, I can see that you are having a wonderful time. But, for me, I have yet to sink my teeth into the meat of this proposal."

"What is there to think about? They need a translator and you can speak the language. There is nothing special or magic about that."

"Well, we shall see. For now, we are on holiday. I know that you are as eager to see the science institute as I am," Anatoly said.

"It will be the highlight of the trip." Irena kissed his cheek and then stepped into a steamy bubble bath. Anatoly had to smile when he heard her let out a relaxing sigh.

Within minutes, the phone rang. It was Mussari. He wanted Anatoly to join him again for dinner. They would discuss the schedule over an intimate meal, just the two of them. Mussari wanted to make sure he had Anatoly's confidence, once and for all. Mussari was not used to having to work this diligently to win someone over, yet he knew he would win. On the other hand, he realized that Anatoly was loyal and not the sort of man who would betray his allegiance. Tonight, he would be closer to a commitment.

Irena called from the tub, "Who was phoning?"

"That was comrade Mussari. He wants me to join him for dinner. I told him I would meet him. Do you mind? He asked that just I attend," Anatoly responded as he gathered his hat and coat.

"Of course not," Irena said, more than content to be left behind to soak in the tub. It had been some time since she had been able to spoil herself. "I'll wait up."

"No need. I can let myself in," Anatoly replied as he walked out the door.

Anatoly took the elevator down to the lobby. Far across the

room, standing with Mussari, were two men who appeared to be of Mussari's ethnic group. Anatoly had not seen them before and their faces bore a solemn look as they spoke. As he drew nearer, he picked up the fact that they spoke Farsi, the language of Iran. Although Anatoly spoke many languages, this was one he had not taken the time to master. Although he couldn't speak the language, he could recognize a word here-and-there, getting the gist of the conversation. It was a detail he decided to keep to himself believing it could be useful down the road. Unfortunately, at this particular moment, he was too far away to hear everything that was being said, but he did pick up the words jihad and fatwa. When Anatoly approached, one of the men made a sudden, nearly indiscernible movement with his eyes which did not go unnoticed by Anatoly. The small group quickly parted and Abu al Mussari was left standing alone. The pleasant smile he always seemed to be wearing reappeared. He held out his hand in welcoming gesture.

"Come, I have reserved a table at a very good restaurant. The car is waiting," Mussari said, as he led Anatoly to the door.

During the ride the restaurant, the men exchanged pleasant small talk discussing their impressions of the flight from Russia, and then their brief glimpse of the city. When they were seated for dinner, Mussari took command of the conversation. He kept squarely on the topic of boxing. He discussed, not only his hope for the future of the team, but the monetary reward that winning would bring. Anatoly listened attentively. Being concerned by the look on the face of his friend, he wanted to ask about the meeting in the lobby, but was not able to interject much as Mussari, purposely, left little room for commentary. Anatoly did not know it, but Mussari's conversation in the hotel was staged specifically for his benefit. Everything Mussari did was premeditated.

After dinner the men sipped on cordials and puffed on expensive cigars, relaxed and satisfied. Mussari knew Anatoly still harbored doubts, but tonight Anatoly's resolve was beginning to weaken.

"So, now you know what I envision for the future. I would like to take a little side trip tonight. I want to show you the facility where the exhibition matches will be held. It is a very nice location, complete with training areas. Our boxers are working out as we speak," Mussari said, looking at his watch.

"I see no reason why not," Anatoly agreed.

With a questioning eyebrow raised, Mussari asked, "Your wife will not be angry with you for coming in late?"

"No. I told her not to wait for me."

"Excellent," Mussari exclaimed. "This will give you an opportunity to try out your skills as translator," he added and then signaled for the waiter. He was pleased to hear that Anatoly could make a decision without including Irena. In his opinion, it was a step in the right direction.

Within the hour, the men entered a modern building. They were met by Gregor, who escorted them through a maze of corridors. They came to a large locker room reserved specifically for the Russian team members. A few men were wandering about, tending to various chores, but most were in the gym, training. Anatoly and Mussari left their coats with Gregor and went in search of the team. They found the men sparring in the gym.

Walking slowly past the German team, Mussari asked in a hushed tone, "Listen closely to the trainer. Can you tell me what advice he is providing?"

Taken aback by the request, Anatoly was at a loss. He thought it irregular to be eavesdropping on the competition's conversation, but since this was just a training session and not a formal bout, he complied. Anatoly figured that Mussari spoke many languages with German being one of them, but now he wasn't so sure. What he didn't know was that Mussari was merely testing him to see if he would comply, and if so, would answer honestly?

Taking care not to make eye contact with the Germans as they walked passed, Anatoly listened. Once they were out of earshot, he responded. "The trainer said, 'Make sure to keep your guard up, that is your weakness. We need to concentrate on that left jab as well, but I can see that your foot work has improved.'"

Mussari nodded, and said "Excellent."

They reached the area where the Russian team was going through their paces, so they stopped to watch. Anatoly was quickly immersed in the experience and Mussari's strange request was pushed to the back of his mind.

Several hours had passed and it was getting very late. Mussari looked at his watch and said, "Comrade, it is time to leave. Tomorrow, I will take you and Irena to the science institute. It will be an early wake up call and another long day."

"Yes, but one Irena has been looking forward to, as I will admit, I have, too," Anatoly replied.

Returning to the hotel, Anatoly entered the room and quietly slid into bed, careful not to disturb a peacefully sleeping Irena.

It seemed as though he had just drifted off when the phone awakened him. It was the front desk with a message from Abu al Mussari. He wished to meet them in the hotel restaurant, in one hour, for breakfast.

Clumsily, Anatoly put the receiver back into the cradle and turned to face Irena. He said, "Are you prepared for a day dedicated to science?"

With a sleep laden smile, Irena said, "I am ready to face anything, at any time, as long as I am with you."

Lightly kissing her lips, Anatoly lumbered to the bathroom in preparation for the day.

The time passed quickly. The Buskeyevs found themselves back in their element as they spent the day discussing physics and nuclear science with many of Germany's top scientists. The day was filled with brilliant minds enjoying a dynamic exchange of ideas. They had in-depth conversations about the Star Wars project which had taken place in the United States. They wondered about the viability of such a scheme and if it could be successful. They all agreed that it looked good, mathematically, but was it realistic? They questioned the financial impact as well as the practicality of it, and decided that it would never make it off of the drawing board.

Their discussions about laser technology didn't stop at the Star Wars project. They considered its uses in the world of communications and medicine. They also discussed the outlook for computers. It was agreed by all that it would be the communication standard of the future. Like the television, and radio before it, the general populace would have at least one system in their home. The versatile machine would be used for generating the news, an assortment of televised programs, and talking to neighbors without picking up the phone. It was inevitable that businesses would not be able to function without a network of them running the company.

It was during their visit to the institution that Irena realized how much she missed the world of academia, a fact she casually mentioned to Anatoly. Mussari, being within earshot, caught the brief exchange between husband and wife, and it gave him a brilliant idea.

Before they knew it, the sun began to set. Mussari apologized for having to call an end to the event, but again the next day would be a long and tedious one. They would have to be up early to get the team ready for the bouts that would be taking place over the next two days. Anatoly's services would be needed for the media as Mussari fully expected the German press to be out in force in anticipation of the coming matches.

Irena shook hands with Professor Geisler, who said, "I'm sorry that the day has ended so soon. I was hoping we could delve deeper into the discussion of quantum physics."

"You have been a gracious host. Perhaps we can return soon and take up where we left off," Irena responded.

"That would be wonderful. You are welcome here any time," Heinz said as he shook Anatoly's hand and bid his guests good night.

During the ride back to the hotel, Anatoly's thoughts went back to Mussari and a question formed in his mind. "You seem to know a lot of people, in many professions, comrade Mussari."

"Does that surprise you? Money is a powerful thing. It creates many opportunities. Doors that would normally be locked become easily accessed," Mussari responded with a gracious smile. He then turned to watch the scenery passing by the window and Anatoly was left to ponder the remark. He had no idea just how many doors Abu al Mussari had easily opened or what kind of power Mussari wielded.

Back in their room, Irena excitedly rattled on, recounting bits of conversation that had taken place earlier in the day. Anatoly listened and was happy that his wife was enjoying her time away from the dreariness of their existence.

Settling down for the night, Irena snuggled beside Anatoly and said thoughtfully, "Tolya, I believe it's time for me to think about a career move. You are thinking about a change. I should consider making one as well."

"My dear wife, you should do whatever makes you happiest," Anatoly said as they lay together in bed. He put his arm around her and they drifted off to sleep.

At breakfast the next morning, the Buskeyevs expected to see Abu al Mussari in anticipation of the boxing exhibitions to be held that day. Instead, Gregor and his wife Natalia greeted them. It was Mussari's desire to have the women spend time sightseeing and shopping while the men tended to the business of the day. Irena had mixed emotions about the new arrangement. Not wanting to impose her opinion to a man she had just met, and one Anatoly was destined to work for, she went long with the plan. She knew that there would be ample opportunity to witness Anatoly acting in his new role as translator. For now, she would have to be patient, something she was not particularly good at.

After breakfast, the women were escorted to a waiting limousine and whisked away to a day filled with whatever their hearts desired, complete with a purse that had no strings. When they parted company, the women went in the direction of the shopping district while the men went in the opposite direction, to the waiting journalists.

• • •

Tim Rausch was an analyst in the Counterintelligence Center at CIA Headquarters in Langley, Virginia. Sitting behind his desk he scrutinized the stack of documents before him. Intelligence had started coming in which seemed to indicate that once quiet terrorist cells were becoming active again. He made notes in his ledger, including any data he deemed to be important, no matter how vague. He had learned over the short time in his position that, sometimes, even the most insignificant chatter could hold invaluable clues.

And so it was on this day. Tim kept a private journal and that little book was with him at all times. The information within the handwritten pages was deliberately concealed. He passed it off as merely his personal observations, anyway. Reading back through his notes, Tim began to piece together a scenario that caused the little hairs on the back of his neck to stand on end. Could this information be correct? How much longer should he wait before putting this data before his supervisors? Not wanting to take anything away from the gravity of the growing threat, Tim thought it best to be patient, a little while longer, anyway. He found out the hard way how sensitive his superiors were to sounding a false alarm. He didn't want to be labeled as a trouble maker.

In an ever growing tide of political correctness, Tim did not discuss the journal with anyone. Besides, he knew that keeping personal data was against the rules. The information in that diary, if it ever got into the wrong hands, could spell disaster, not only for the agency, but for the agents in the field as well. Tim was well aware of the regulations, and the consequences should he be found out, but from day one had completely disregarded them.

A handsome man, Tim stood just over six feet tall. His wavy dark brown hair was still thick, but he had found a few strands of errant gray scattered throughout. His brown eyes were alive with intelligence, and starting to show signs of age. As much as he hated to admit it, he needed reading glasses, something he had been putting off.

Another thing that had been neglected of late was his overall health. His athletic physique was in desperate need of a workout. When his schedule permitted, Tim enjoyed playing sports. Basketball, tennis, and an occasional round of golf, were high on his list of leisure activities. These days, with the growing unrest in the world, his work at the CIA took up most of his free time. Relaxation was something of a luxury, but he knew that had to be remedied, and quickly. If what he read in the reports was real, and he had no reason to believe that it wasn't, he would need to be in shape to stave off whatever might be coming.

And something was coming …

Under the rules imposed by top government officials, agencies such as the CIA and FBI could not exchange information, no matter how significant, regarding persons of interest. The CIA was responsible for surveillance outside of the United States, while the FBI monitored activities within. If an individual from a foreign country, on the CIA's "watch list," entered the United States, the CIA was helpless in communicating that information (without a court order and probable cause) to their counterparts within the FBI. This was an increasing cause of frustration to many of the analysts and field agents, not only within the CIA, but in many government agencies. Tim took the job of protecting his country very seriously, and this rule had hampered his agency's ability to be proactive, especially when getting the courts involved.

Tim had a habit of taking everything to heart, no matter how unimportant, but in his division, upper management seemed to be more interested in climbing the ladder than taking care of agency business.

Tim sat back in his chair. He put his mind to work as he thought about the terror organizations around the world. al Qaeda was definitely a growing threat. The mastermind behind that organization, Osama bin Laden, was someone Tim had been keeping a watchful eye on. He recalled the 1992 attack in Yemen which specifically targeted the American military. The soldiers were in Yemen on an international famine relief effort when al Qaeda detonated two bombs. Their sole intent was to kill the Americans. However, the plan was flawed because the Americans were not staying at the intended hotel. Consequently, no American was injured, much less killed, in the blast. Back in the U.S., that attempt had barely been a blip on the radar, but Tim thought it valuable information and had put the details in his journal.

Then, in February of 1993, another attack came against the U.S. and this time, it was not on foreign soil. This attack was at home, in the form of a car bomb. It was a 1500 pound urea nitrate-hydrogen gas enhanced device that had been parked in the underground garage of the World Trade Center in New York City. The purpose of that bomb, he learned later, was to knock the North Tower into the South Tower bringing both structures down, thus annihilating thousands of people and leaving massive destruction in its wake. Fortunately for the towers, the architect had built the structure soundly and it withstood the massive blast.

Armed with the details, and based upon the intelligence he had been receiving regarding al Qaeda, Tim had tried in vain to circumvent a catastrophe before it happened. He remembered the conversation he had had with Stan Jeffries, his supervisor, who admonished him again.

"We've had this conversation before, Rausch. How many times do I have to tell you? We're never going to be able to build a bridge between the CIA and the FBI. They've made it crystal clear. There will be no follow-through of persons of interest after they enter the U.S. According to the Constitution, once they're here, they are afforded the same rights and protection that you and I have."

Visibly agitated, Tim responded. "Aw, come on, Stan. You know as well as I do, these guys are up to no good. Do we have to take a hit before someone will do something?"

"You're going to get us fired if you keep this up, you know that," Stan stated none too gently.

"Mark my words, Stan, you're going to be reading about Ramzi Yousef and his band of conspirators, and sooner rather than later. I'm sure of it," Tim said over his shoulder as he walked out of Stan's office, frustrated, yet again.

How right he had been. In March of 1994, four men were convicted of carrying out the attack. However, Ramzi Yousef and another man, Eyad Ismoil, were still in prison awaiting their day in court.

While he was thinking, Tim pulled his journal from his briefcase. Flipping through the pages he found references to Hezbollah and Hamas, both with deep roots in Islam. Their sole intent has been the eradication of the Israeli people and, in recent years, the American infidels.

Yes, things were definitely happening in the Middle East … things that needed to be monitored, and closely.

Tim hurried home from a busy day at the office. An avid fan of boxing, he didn't want to miss the satellite broadcast of the exhibition fights that were being held in Germany that night. With the advent of satellite television he would be able to see many of the sporting events not shown on the local cable network. It was one of the main reasons he bought the dish. He particularly liked the newfound freedom satellite television provided in viewing options, and even though he had to pay extra for some programs, he didn't mind. After a stressful day at work, he enjoyed kicking back in his favorite lounge chair in front of the television and blocking out the events of the day. He told himself that soon, he would take advantage of the new gym that had opened around the corner, but for tonight, he would watch as others worked out.

As usual, Tim's wife, Donna, and their two kids, met him at the door. Scott was a robust seven year old who loved to play sports. He had dark brown hair, a pug nose and gray eyes that sparkled whenever given a chance to discuss his latest at bat or football goal. Krista was a freckle-faced six going on sixteen. Donna referred to her as the ultimate drama queen to which Tim would reply, "Just like her mother," much to Donna's displeasure. Tim listened patiently as each one of his children excitedly gave detailed descriptions of their day.

Donna always let the children go first. When it finally was her turn, and looking past her at the picture on the television,

Tim said, "Hon, do you mind if we talk a little later? I was really hoping to catch some of these interviews."

"Sure," Donna replied flatly. Here we go again, she thought, and then with sarcasm, said, "The kids and I are going to the dining room. You know … the dining room? It's the place where normal families go to eat their supper together."

Keeping his eyes glued to the tube, Tim quietly took his usual pace in front of the television. When he didn't respond, Donna turned to go.

"If you get hungry and feel like joining us, you know where the kitchen is or you can eat out here," Donna muttered as she strode down the empty hallway, and then added sarcastically, "Like you normally do."

As Donna walked away she could hear Tim's muffled response, "I'll get something a little later."

All of Tim's attention was fixed on the interview taking place on his television screen. There were two men. One was a translator and the other someone Tim assumed was a promoter. Who are those guys? Tim questioned himself, but came up short. The ticker across the bottom of the screen identified the men as Anatoly Buskeyev and Abu al Mussari. He immediately thought, what in the world is a Russian doing in Germany hanging around with a man clearly from the Middle East? Something didn't jive and Tim was all about making the puzzle pieces fit. Something here definitely didn't feel right. Trying to justify things in his own mind, he decided that, since Russia was no longer a Communist country, men were trying their hand at entrepreneurial endeavors. After further contemplation he knew that boxing certainly was a lucrative sport. He filed the questions, as well as their names, in the back of his mind for later entry into his journal, and then settled down for an evening of sport.

• • •

The office was cold and dark. The same shortages that affected Anatoly's household had begun to appear at work or so it seemed. He flipped the light switch, but to no avail. Looking at the thermostat on the wall, the temperature inside was nearly as cold as it was outside. He had come to the conclusion; it was time to leave his government post.

With a weary sigh, Anatoly sat behind his desk. A few moments later, Vladimir Chechenko, a worker Anatoly had known for many years knocked on the door. He said that a decision had been made to cycle off the power over the weekend in an effort to conserve. Anatoly had to laugh at that comment knowing it would take more energy to regain a comfortable temperature than letting it run during the down times to maintain a reasonable environment. A few moments later, the power returned and the lights, as well as the heat, came on.

Reaching into his coat pocket, Anatoly felt a small piece of paper and wondered how it had gotten there. It contained Abu al Mussari's name and phone number. Many questions ran through his mind, but rather than sit and contemplate each one, he placed a call instead. Mussari answered on the first ring.

Not completely sure why he called, Anatoly hesitated before responding, but Mussari patiently waited. Finally, getting his thoughts in order, a troubled Anatoly said, "Well comrade, I believe I have decided that leaving my post is in my, and Irena's, best interest."

"That's wonderful," Mussari exclaimed, and then added, "tonight we celebrate. I will pick you up at seven o'clock sharp."

"I will give my resignation; however I don't feel like I can just walk out and leave without making sure that there is someone of integrity and intelligence to take my place. I realize that this facility will be closing soon, but it certainly deserves to have a respectable and timely retirement."

That played right into Mussari's hands as he still had to fulfill his prime objective, one in which Anatoly was not yet aware. "Comrade, I know you are an honorable man and I would not ask you to do something that goes against your principles. We will talk more tonight at dinner. I cannot tell you how pleased I am that you have decided to join our cause."

"I'm not sure I understand," Anatoly stated, consciously aware of an unknown dread.

"Why, making the Russian Boxing Federation the best in the world," Mussari exclaimed with an easy laugh.

After ending the call with Mussari, Anatoly found a small box. Placing it on his desk, he began the process of removing his personal belongings. In doing so, he felt a brief moment of loss. At least that's what he attributed it to. Looking around his office he realized that there was more here than he had anticipated (including memories), but then, he had spent most of his adult life working for the state. It had taken years to accumulate, so now he would take his time removing it. There was no rush to empty the office.

As he mindlessly placed pictures and assorted memorabilia in the box, Anatoly's thoughts drifted back to the conversation he just ended. Mussari said that he understood the reasoning behind the slow retreat. That certainly should have made Anatoly feel better. He wondered why he didn't feel better, but chalked it up to separation anxiety or perhaps to the fear of the unknown.

As Anatoly fretted over leaving his post, Abu al Mussari

smiled in victory. Each piece of the puzzle was falling neatly into place. Even though he could sense Anatoly's hesitation, this latest incident only served to convince him that Anatoly was the correct choice. He picked up his phone, called to have his private jet ready on a moments notice, and then called Qusay Sharaf in Dubai.

Allah was great indeed.

The restaurant was alive with music and laughter. Abu al Mussari, Anatoly, and Irena were seated at a table tucked in a dark corner, away from the noise and bustle of the lively crowd. Mussari chose this particular place because he knew it would be loud. He wanted to be sure their voices would not be overheard by anyone nearby should the conversation turn in a direction that would require privacy.

Anatoly was surprised at the number of people at the restaurant considering how bad the economy had become, a statement he had made to his host.

In response, Mussari said, "Yes, the economy is bad … for some. Not everyone in Russia is suffering, as you can plainly see."

Drinks were served and dinner followed close behind. While they ate conversation was light, and covered a variety of topics. Then, when the last of the meal was cleared away, Mussari said, "Comrades, I have a request to make of you. That is, if you are agreeable."

Noticing the grave look upon Mussari's face, Irena responded first. "What is it that we can do for you?"

"Yes, please let us know what we can do. You have been so generous, even knowing the possibility existed that I might not want to take the position you had offered," Anatoly said, his eyes level with Mussari's.

Mussari let out a short, dry, almost forced laugh. "It isn't as bad as all that. There is someone I would like for you to meet; therefore, I would like for you to accompany me to Dubai."

Thinking that was a strange request, and coming out of the blue, Anatoly was ready to question the point when, looking from Anatoly to Mussari and back again, Irena interjected, lightheartedly, "Oh, that would be lovely. I see no reason why we couldn't go, do you, Anatoly?"

Taken by surprise at Irena's bold response, Anatoly raised his eyebrows and said, "No, of course not."

"Wonderful! Then I will make the necessary arrangements. As you know, I have contacts in the right places, so I was able to get the necessary papers for you. Since I had to get visas for the trip to Germany, I took the liberty of securing the proper documents for Dubai. How soon can you leave?"

Staring in disbelief, Anatoly said, "I will need a couple of days, no more. There are arrangements to be made at work."

"Yes, of course," the ever-agreeable Mussari replied.

As promised, the papers were delivered. Anatoly made sure his responsibilities were in order as he and Irena, once again, found themselves on board a lavish private jet. They landed in just under four hours and were escorted to a waiting limousine that whisked them away to a modern high-rise in the heart of the city.

Change was well under way in this burgeoning metropolis. Construction was taking place everywhere they looked. There was no doubt in Anatoly's mind that big things were happening in this part of the world.

The limousine came to a slow stop in the front of a

luxurious high rise. At first Anatoly thought it was a hotel, but upon closer inspection, he realized it was a condominium. While the driver unloaded suitcases, Abu al Mussari led the Buskeyevs into the lobby and then to the elevator.

The doors slid open and they entered the lift. Mussari depressed a button and the motor hummed as they traveled silently up the shaft to a meeting that would forever change the course of history.

• • •

Feeling restless, Tim pushed the chair away from his desk and stood next to the window. He pounded the top of a pack of cigarettes against the palm of his hand. He took one, placed it between his teeth and lit it. Inhaling deeply, he made a face and exhaled while looking at the smoldering end before stubbing it out. With his arms folded across his chest, he looked out onto the street. Questions had been brewing in his mind ever since he watched that interview on television with Abu al Mussari and Anatoly Buskeyev. Looking into the distance, he tried to "see" what his mind was telling him.

Tim's search for the names Buskeyev and Mussari brought some results, but the way the pieces fit together made him quite uncomfortable. There was very little new information on Mussari, and always sketchy at best, a fact that didn't surprise him. Searches pointed to Abu al Mussari being a Hezbollah operative, at least that's what the intelligence had indicated, but his life prior to Hezbollah was non-existent. It was like the man didn't exist until the day he joined leagues with Hezbolla. Tim figured that, either Mussari had his history erased or they provided him with a new identity.

On the other side of the coin, he had Anatoly Buskeyev, and Anatoly's wife, Irena. They were premiere scientists in the former Soviet Union. Tim had to wonder. Which of the two could Mussari be interested in? Was it Irena with her intimate knowledge of nuclear power? Could it be Anatoly and his direct connection to the Russian arsenal? Or perhaps it was both? Trying to unravel the maze of questions, Tim's immediate reaction was that Mussari was planning to take these two scientists out of Russia, but that created a whole new list of questions. Would it be with weapons, or with the intention of using their knowledge to create a weapon someplace else? He had no way of knowing, so it was at this juncture that he took the data to his superiors, even though he was operating on a hunch, with the hopes of getting some collaborative support.

Tim took a seat offered to him. His intention was to maintain control of the conversation, so he cut right to the chase. "Good morning, Stan. I've been trying to get information on a Hezbollah big shot by the name of Abu al Mussari. He's been recruiting talent in Russia because he knows that there are lots of pissed off party 'favorites,' who are now nobodies, in the hopes of getting his hands on weapons. I think he's working a couple of marks, a husband and wife team. They both know far too much for Mussari to be hanging around with them as just drinking buddies. He has them running around Germany, and probably some other places, on some sort of boxing junket." Tim stopped when Stan interjected a grunt, but when Stan didn't offer any input, Tim continued. "I really don't like it. I've had some interesting crosstalk with our guys in Near Eastern and South Asian Analysis shops, as well as the folks in the Russian and European Analysis group. From what we can gather, this guy, Mussari, is communicating with some bad guys here in the U.S., but I can't get anything from the FBI regarding telephone intercepts that they may have here at home." As soon as the words took form, Tim knew he had overstepped his boundaries.

"We've had this conversation before, Tim, over and over it seems. Reno is adamant regarding keeping this separation between foreign and internal intelligence. I've tried talking to the Deputy Director, at your request I might add, and as far as he's concerned, it's a 'No Go,'" Stan reiterated.

Pleading his case, Tim said, "Stan, I'm really concerned that this bad-ass is building a network here, and I'm scared to death that he's working some sort of serious weapons transfer deal."

"There will be no coordination of any kind between you and any other agency. Do I make myself clear?" Stan exclaimed.

"Yes, sir."

"And I don't want to hear any complaints from the FBI that you are developing contacts, and going around Reno's directives. Got it?" Stan repeated with authority.

A hardheaded pragmatist, Tim answered boldly, "Yeah sure, I got it. But, you have got to know that this is some really dangerous shit, Stan. You know I've been on this guy, Mussari's, ass for some time now, and I get a real bad feeling when I see him recruiting in Russia, and trying to make contacts here."

"Look, I hear what you're saying, Tim, but it is what it is, and you should know that by now." Looking at his watch, Stan said, "I have a meeting in ten minutes that I have to prepare for, so will you leave me to it?"

"Okay, sorry boss," Tim replied over his shoulder, leaving Stan to his paperwork.

Sitting behind his desk again, Tim looked into the distance, envisioning the white dome of the Capitol rising majestically on the horizon. He shook his head to clear the scenarios of devastation and annihilation playing out in his mind.

• • •

The elevator came to a halt near the topmost floor of the high-rise. When the door slid open Mussari and the Buskeyevs were standing in a small foyer which immediately opened into a vast expanse of a room. The grand entrance was decorated with very expensive artifacts and modern furniture. In the undercurrent of the atmosphere there emanated a soft aroma of jasmine and everything was as clean and precise as a museum exhibit. Taking a tentative step forward, Irena moved in the direction of the windows which spanned the length of the room, and overlooked the open sea. The view took her breath away.

"What do you think of my friend's home?" Abu al Mussari asked, his face taking on the familiar, friendly smile.

Barely able to take her eyes from the bluest water and cleanest, white, beaches she had ever seen, Irena had to force herself to face Mussari.

"This place is beyond my wildest imaginings. It is too beautiful to put into words," Irena said, mesmerized by the scenery.

Taking his place by her side, Anatoly put his arm around Irena's waist and said, "I must agree with you, my dear. I don't think I have ever seen anything like this. A photograph would not do justice to this vista."

"Paradise?" Mussari interjected. "Come then, let us go for a walk. You can get an idea of just how magnificent this place truly is. As you can plainly see, it is growing. Soon, it will rival the retreats of the rich and famous, and they will come from the word over to partake of Dubai's generosity. This will be the place they will come to get away from it all," Mussari exclaimed as he ushered them to the door and back out onto the street.

It was late afternoon and the sidewalk was bustling with the comings and goings of people in their everyday life. Anatoly watched the eyes of the passersby and noticed that they all seemed to share the same contented look. Suddenly, he felt the desire to become one of them. The *joie de vivre* was contagious.

And while Anatoly watched the locals, Mussari kept his eye on Anatoly. His little outing was having the desired effect. He knew that the past few years, pent up in a stuffy office, barely scraping by on insufficient wages, Anatoly was ripe for a change in his life, and Dubai would offer him that refuge.

Finally, after an hour of walking, Mussari said, "My friend, Qusay, should be home by now. We should go back and ready ourselves for dinner."

Qusay met them at the door when they returned from their short trek around the neighborhood. There were many questions on Anatoly's mind, but he decided to hold on to them. He knew there would be ample time for discussion later.

Abu al Mussari made the formal introductions and Qusay then showed the Buskeyevs to their room where they were given some time to relax and unwind. Then, at eight O'clock sharp, everyone was to meet in the library for cocktails before an informal dinner.

"I wish for my guests to be comfortable, so please, dress casually while in my home," Qusay said as he quietly closed the door and left them.

Irena was at a complete loss for words, which was very unusual for her. Anatoly just smiled as he watched her facial expressions change from awe and wonder to complete surrender. Just when he figured she was going to say something, her half opened mouth snapped closed, with the thought never taking shape.

Laughing, Anatoly said, "My dear, you may as well get used to this sort of thing. I get the impression that, with my new job responsibility, there will be more of this lifestyle in our future."

"Who do you think this Qusay is?" Irena asked, slipping off her shoes.

"That is a very good question. No one ever mentioned what he does or who he is. All we were given was his name. However, I am sure we will find out in good time. Be patient, my dear wife," Anatoly replied. He found the bathroom and readied the shower. In contrast to Moscow, it was quite hot outdoors and he had worked up a sweat in their earlier wanderings.

Irena slid out of her dress, and in her slip lay down on the bed while Anatoly showered. Her thoughts ran wild as she tried to come to some sort of conclusion as to why Anatoly and why now? She knew that Anatoly's job was in a government agency that did not warranty easy access.

She was soon to find out.

At the appointed hour the Buskeyevs casually strolled into the library where they found Qusay and Mussari with a drink in hand, heavy in conversation. They were speaking in hushed tones, in their native language of Farsi, in much the same manner as Anatoly had found Mussari in the lobby of the hotel in Germany with the two unknown men. When Mussari noticed the Buskeyevs standing in the doorway, the conversation immediately reverted to Russian. Little did Anatoly know, but this conversation, as well as the one in Germany, had been staged for his benefit.

In the short time that he had observed the two men together, Anatoly concluded that Abu al Mussari was decidedly in command. He had an air of patience (as well as an underlying deviousness) about him that Anatoly likened to a street urchin. Mussari clearly wanted something. That much Anatoly surmised by the dogged nature with which he was being pursued. But to what end, that was the question.

When Qusay offered his guests a drink, Mussari began questioning Irena. "What do you think of Dubai?"

"I think this is a lovely place. The ocean … the beaches … this luxurious condominium, so high up, and the view is spectacular," Irena responded with a demure smile.

"Then, it should come as no surprise that the leadership of this country must change course if they want to maintain their current status in the world economies. Naturally, oil is the export which bought them to this point; however, their oil supplies will not last forever, and with demands around the world ever growing, they will run out sooner than later."

Irena agreed. "I never really thought about it, but it must be true. Countries once considered to be third world are starting to come into their own. More people are driving cars and populations are growing. Of course, that makes perfect sense."

"And with that growth comes the desire to educate. Dubai wishes to expand their universities. Consequently, they are in the market for highly skilled professors. I was thinking that you, Irena, would fit in that setting quite nicely," Mussari stated reassuringly.

Irena looked at Anatoly, her eyes wide with pleasure. Then, turning to speak to Mussari, Irena said, "I would love the opportunity to investigate this option more. Once Anatoly removes himself from his position at the depot, there would be nothing to keep us in Moscow."

While Irena and Mussari were discussing future possibilities, Anatoly noticed that Qusay's look had become grave. When Anatoly asked how he was feeling, Qusay remarked, "I feel fine, at least as well as can be expected."

"What do you mean? Are you ill?" Anatoly asked, and the concern for his host was evident in his tone.

"No, that is not it. I grieve because my people suffer," Qusay remarked.

"Please, Qusay," Mussari interjected quickly.

Directing his response to Mussari, Anatoly said, "I'm sorry, I'm afraid I don't understand?"

Qusay looked around the room at the faces before him, and knew this was the reason he had been brought here. It was his responsibility to open the door and lay the foundation in order for Mussari to close the deal.

In the back of his mind, something told Anatoly that this was it. He was about to find out the reason he and Irena had been brought to Dubai.

Seeming to ignore Mussari's rebuke, Qusay continued. "Are you familiar with Iran, comrade Buskeyev?"

"I know a little of your country. In what manner are you inquiring?" Anatoly asked, taking the drink being offered.

Qusay responded with another question. "Geographically speaking, are you familiar?"

"Of course I am familiar. Iran's borders are flanked by many countries. Some are much smaller …"

Interrupting Anatoly's response, Qusay exclaimed, "Smaller, yes. But they carry in their hand a mighty sword, and one which my country cannot hope to fight against."

"At least not in this day and age," Mussari countered. "And, even if they started today, on a program to counter an attack, should one come, it would be years, perhaps even decades, before Iran could defend itself in modern warfare. Then, it would be too late."

"I'm afraid I don't follow you," Anatoly replied, but in his heart, he knew where this dialogue was headed. In reality, he had known all along, but had opted to ignore his instincts.

"As you know, Israel is no friend of the Arab world. Sitting between Israel and Iran is Iraq, which as you know, is currently on very shaky ground. And it is that very same ground which embraces the hand of Israel. I speak of the greatest Satan of all, the United States of America. Both America and Israel have weapons that, with one blow, could wipe Iran off the face of the earth."

Considering Mussari's words, and shaking his head in denial, Anatoly responded with conviction, "I do not believe that the people of the United States would allow such a thing to happen."

Doing his best to convince Anatoly, Mussari asked a pointed question. "How can you defend them, considering your countries have been archenemies for decades?"

"Because, I believe that the people of the United States are decent human beings, just the same as any Russian or Iranian citizen for that matter. They would be outraged if their government unleashed a bomb against your country without provocation or cause."

"How can you be so sure?" Mussari quizzed, his eyes narrowed, questioning.

"I have faith in humankind," Anatoly responded simply yet boldly.

"Let me ask you this, then: Are not the government officials of the United States elected by those very people that you are defending?"

"Yes, I suppose they are." Anatoly had to admit, Mussari had a valid point, but he was still not convinced.

With passion in his voice, Qusay added, "And the United States has shown what great a Satan it truly is. Has it not already devastated an enemy with nuclear weapons, not once, but twice? To my mind, and the minds of many Middle Easterners, that is justification enough. If the government of the United States, or that of Israel, or any other country within striking distance, launched an attack, we would be unable to defend ourselves against that sort of power."

Irena, who had been quietly listening up to that point, finally interjected a question. "What are you proposing, comrade?"

"The sale of a nuclear weapon to our comrades in Iran," was the curt reply, but it was Anatoly, and not their hosts, who responded, and his eyes were firmly affixed to those of Mussari.

Trying to break the disquiet that had developed in the room, Qusay implored, "Please, try to understand. Put yourself in our shoes. We are defenseless against anyone who would want to do us harm. What we ask is for a weapon to protect our wives, our sons and daughters. This is no more than what you ask of your government. Yet, while the world grows ever more dangerous, a peace-loving Iran sits, an easy target for those looking to conquer."

"Surely you don't think that a nuclear bomb can just disappear?" Anatoly asked, waving his hand in the air. He figured his host must have that part of the plan figured out. He was also interested in hearing how Mussari planed to go about getting such a dangerous weapon out of Russia, and then what he would do with it once it was in his control.

Just as Mussari was preparing to give an answer, they were summoned to dinner. The group exited the library and followed the servant to the dining room. Everyone was seated comfortably, their meals placed before them, but there was very little talk.

Choosing his words very carefully, Mussari broke the uneasy

silence. "I must apologize for my friend, Qusay. As you have learned, he is a man of passion and, being Iranian, he loves his country. He is concerned about the hatred that has been unjustifiably aimed at the Arab nations. He is merely anxious, as we all are, watching events around the world as they unfold. Whoever decides to help Iran with this mighty task will be compensated handsomely, I assure you. So, that being said let us not ruin our wonderful dinner with such apocalyptic talk. Please, everyone, enjoy your food."

Picking up on his queue, Qusay remarked offhandedly, "I am told the monetary rewards would be extraordinary, as much as three million American dollars for one weapon."

Mussari watched Irena's face when the dollar amount was mentioned. He noticed that she tried, but could not conceal her amazement. By the mere fact that she was trying to keep her emotions hidden, Mussari had to sweeten the pot. As he passed the basket of bread to Irena, he pounced. "It is no secret, at least to my eyes, that you are quite partial to Qusay's home away from home. Am I correct in that assessment?"

Keeping her eyes veiled, Irena responded, "Oh, yes. I don't think I have seen anything quite like it."

Again, Qusay interjected as required, "Then, I would gladly transfer the title of this place to the name of Buskeyev. For one who would risk so much for my people, it is the least I could do."

As the conversation went on between Irena and Mussari, something had piqued Anatoly's curiosity. "Why would you be willing to pay in American dollars?"

Without missing a beat, Mussari provided a sound answer. "As you know, Russian currency is not worth much in the world market today. Dollars are strong and recognized everywhere."

This explanation sounded quite reasonable to Anatoly, so he blindly accepted it. He then bumped Irena's leg under the table to change the direction of the conversation, as he was very uncomfortable in the way it was currently going. Irena, being the dutiful spouse, did not utter another word, and talk of blood money faded. Meanwhile, Abu al Mussari knew the real reason for paying with American currency, and that was to deflect any traceability back to Russia, and subsequently, Hezbollah. Once the bombs were detonated, the money trail would be difficult to follow. But the *coup de maître* was the fact they were paying for the demise of Satan, and his followers, with his own money. Mussari laughed to himself at the irony.

Dinner dragged on and conversation was strained. Anatoly waited, half expecting Mussari to bring up the topic of armaments and compensation again at some point during the long hour it took to complete the four course meal, but Mussari had other intentions. He wanted to let the Buskeyevs mull it over in their own minds during dinner, and then together in their bedchamber later that night. From what he knew of Irena, she would be the catalyst in persuading Anatoly that helping Iran achieve nuclear independence would be the right thing to do. She had proven that she was all about money and status. She certainly was not as upstanding and conscientious as her husband. As far as Mussari was concerned that was an added, and welcome benefit. He didn't realize that it would take this long or be this difficult to convince Anatoly. But, now he was very close to striking a deal. It would be a great day when he could finally make the call to the Supreme Cultural Revolution Council to tell them of his success.

After everyone had finished their supper, Mussari said,

"Come, let us take a walk along the beach. There is a cool breeze tonight and the moon is full. Look, can you see how it reflects upon the water?"

"Yes, like diamonds," Irena replied, but Anatoly did not care for the look in her eyes.

"Let me get your wrap, my dear," Anatoly said flatly, and walked to their room to get her shawl.

Later that night, after they had lain together quietly for some time, Irena said, "Speak to me Tolya. You've been so quiet tonight. What is on your mind?"

"You know what is on my mind. Why do you have to ask such a foolish question?"

"Because, you are not talking to me. How can I help if you don't talk?" Irena replied with a slight pout.

"What can you possibly help with? That man wants to buy a nuclear bomb, Irena, and he thinks I can sell him one. Doesn't that concern you? Imagine what something that powerful, in the wrong hands, could do," Anatoly stated solemnly.

"Oh Tolya, do you believe, after all the time you have spent with Abu al Mussari, that his are the wrong hands? You heard Qusay speak of his country … and the way his people care about their families. These men are no different from Russians in that regard. Think about the children, Tolya." When Anatoly didn't respond, Irena tried another tactic. "Imagine if it had been the other way around and you were doing the asking. Would you want Mussari to think yours were the wrong hands?"

"Really, Irena, how can I not consider everything you just mentioned? Yes, they have reason to be concerned. And of course I understand their plight. But, I am also smart enough to realize the consequences of my deeds. We all have choices in life, my dear. What if I agree and it's the wrong choice?"

"What if you don't agree and they are attacked? How would you feel then? Remember, Mussari did say that someone would help them." Imploring now, Irena said, "Tolya … why not us? You heard what comrade Mussari said of compensation. Think of it!"

Irena's words echoed in Anatoly's ears. He was thinking of it. Only that little voice was there again, in his head, telling him that he was being played. But, then he thought of Irena, their meager flat in Moscow, their tattered clothes, and how thin she had become due to stress and lack of an adequate diet. He closed his eyes and said a little prayer to all the gods he could think of, asking for divine guidance. But, at the end of the day, he knew that there was only one person who could make the final decision, and that was he.

Kissing Irena's forehead softly, Anatoly bid her goodnight.

While Anatoly was struggling with one of the most important decisions of his life, Tim was studying the material lying before him on the desk. As he searched through the archives for information on Mussari and Buskeyev, he found various articles which generated some interesting data on Abu al Mussari. Taking major points from various articles, Tim began jotting observations in his journal as he read:

1992: Although some of the meeting notes have not been verified, it appears Hezbollah feels they can recruit former high-level military and scientific officers in Russia. The hardships endured by the people, due to the collapse of the former Soviet Union, would make some of them prime targets.

Knowing this, Hezbollah operatives (Abu al Mussari?) would be tasked specifically to identify the crème of the crop.

Council member's interest:

Weapons miniaturization initiatives developed through KGB intelligence efforts in the U.S.

Recruit one or more officials of rank within the Russian Nuclear Storage and Maintenance Facility (Nikolai Popov; Anatoly Buskeyev)

There it was. The connection Tim had been looking for. He turned his attention back to the papers in front of him. While he had been engrossed in reading, a thought about Mussari had crossed his mind. Tim was becoming increasingly aware of Abu al Mussari. From what he could determine, Mussari had been involved in many attacks throughout the world.

Stopping for a moment, Tim's thoughts went back to the interview, before the boxing match that he had watched just weeks earlier. He knew now what he had figured all along, that Abu al Mussari was no businessman, at least not in the literal sense of the word. Tim knew Mussari had to be up to no good. He jotted a few more notes in his journal:

Abu al Mussari and Anatoly Buskeyev: nuclear relationship —yes-

Russia's miniaturization program and Irena Buskeyev; convenient connection; two for one?

Follow up with weapons group. Has Hezbollah recently purchased a missile launcher from the North Koreans? If so, would the range be adequate to reach Israel from Iran?

Putting the pieces together, Tim knew he had to alert his superiors. His fear was that Abu al Mussari was poised to buy a nuke. But, then he considered how the conversation would play out. Knowing he still didn't have a whole lot to go on, he continued his investigation into Abu al Mussari and the group known as Hezbollah.

Later that evening, before going home, Tim stopped at the Foaming Brew, a seedy little bar that he and longtime friend, Bob Rizsko, frequented.

Bob worked for the National Capital Region Council of Governments as a Senior Healthcare Policy Advisor. Tim had known Bob since high school and they had formed a solid friendship which had not faltered over the years. They would often meet to discuss the state of political affairs in the U.S and around the world.

Bob was the brother Tim never had. They both were fairly conservative in their political views and put God and country up at the top of the list right along with family. They stood up for each other at their weddings, and Bob was the one friend that Donna didn't mind Tim hanging out with. Living on the other side of town, Bob's wife JaNelle and their two kids, Bobby Junior and Heather, were not close to Tim's family; however, they always spent Thanksgiving and Christmas together, alternating between the two holidays.

Tim decided to fill Bob in on what he had learned knowing he could trust Bob completely.

After considering Tim's words, Bob asked, "So, you think we should be worried about this group, Hezbollah?" Looking for their waitress, and then making eye contact, Bob waved her to the table for another round of drinks.

"Yes, I believe they are a force to be reckoned with and should not be ignored. They have a lot of financial backing and all the earmarks associated with a fanatical separatist organization. My fear is that they're embedding cells here, in the U.S.," Tim said declining another beer and the waitress left.

"Well, if anyone would have a handle on things, it would be you. Keep an eye on 'em, pal. Don't let the bureaucrats get you down." When Tim didn't order another beer, Bob tried to get the attention of the waitress again, saying, "Hey, don't be wimping out on me. Let me get you another brewski; my treat."

Shaking his head and putting his hand up to stop his friend from acting further, Tim said, "No thanks, I've still got over half of this one. I'm good."

After pondering Tim's earlier conversation regarding terrorist activities around the world, Bob started to consider the consequences of an attack on the United States. He said, "You know, as a country, we used to have our shit pretty together regarding, say, a major attack or a pandemic. Did you know that we used to have nearly two thousand 'Packaged Disaster Hospitals' situated around the country. Each one of those mobile units had two hundred beds and a thirty day supply of consumables. There were three operating sections, a lab and X-ray station, along with a generator in case power was intermittent, and they even had their own water reservoirs. What in the hell happened to the days when we worried about someone or something encroaching upon our sovereignty and taking us out?"

Rolling the beer bottle between his hands, Tim said, "I don't know, Bob. I've been wondering the same thing myself here lately."

Continuing in his no-nonsense manner, Bob said, "By that same token, today there are no mobile hospitals, no portable operatories, no X-ray stations, and no generators dedicated to disaster hospital use."

"What do we have? Anything?" Tim asked as he listened in disbelief.

"Oh, sure … let's see … we have 20,000 cots, but no real provisions to go with them, only enough supplies to sustain your basic first aid. If something terrible happened in this country, we would be completely and utterly unprepared. My God, think about it, pal. 20,000 cots! That's it. One major event in any city in this country and boom, those cots are gone," Bob exclaimed in frustration.

"Well, like you said, I'm going to be keeping my eye on this bunch. They're making the tiny hairs on the back of my neck stand up. I don't like the way it smells," Tim said reaching for his keys.

The men parted company, and as they went to their respective homes, each was hoping that the scenarios playing out in their mind's eye would never come to pass.

• • •

In the early hours of the morning, Anatoly rolled out of bed. He stood by the window, high above the ground and looked out at the black sky reflected in the ocean. The moonlight played upon the water, its light flickering on the tips of the waves moving in hypnotic rhythm. He had not closed his eyes all night as he battled with endless questions tearing at his moral fiber. Every time he thought one question had been conquered, two more would raise their ugly head.

Unable to take it any longer, Anatoly climbed out of bed in the hopes of clearing his mind. At that moment, and silently berating himself, he realized that the boxing offer was nothing more than a ruse, merely a way to get to him. But, even with that knowledge, he found a way to justify Mussari's tactics. "After all, asking someone to sell such a powerful weapon is not a simple thing to do," he told himself, although he still didn't believe it. That calm, secure feeling of relief, which normally follows making a decision as important as this, was missing.

As he listened to Irena's steady breathing he thought of all the wonderful things they could do with the rest of their lives if they had a little money tucked away and were living in a paradise such as Dubai appeared to be. Irena was seriously considering the offer of working in the Science Department at the Dubai University. He turned to look at his peacefully sleeping wife, and wondered what dreams were playing out behind her lovely eyelids. Taking a deep breath, he knew what he had to do.

Using an old religious ritual, Anatoly made a sign of the cross upon his chest, and then slid quietly between the sheets. He took the utmost care not to disturb his wife. He drifted off and slept the last few hours until dawn.

When Anatoly awoke the sun was beaming in the window. Irena was up, and in the bathroom, preparing for another day. Feeling lighter than he had in months, Anatoly put his arms behind his head and studied the ceiling. Looking around the room he realized that this must be the master suite. The sheer size of the room, and the location within the condo, had drawn him to that conclusion. He also realized he could easily live here. Then the questions came. How many others had been lured here only to decide in the end to return home instead of agreeing with the plan? Trying to ignore the voices arguing within his mind, he squelched them. He had made his decision. There would be no going back.

Irena emerged wearing a pair of earth toned linen slacks and a bright green silk blouse, unbuttoned just daringly enough to reveal ample cleavage. Her brown hair was combed back, loosely held by a barrette, making her face appear much younger than her years.

"Come Anatoly, get up," Irena said playfully. "I am sure comrade Mussari is awaiting our arrival for breakfast."

"Your wish is my command, Czarina," Anatoly replied, and playfully slapped her behind as he passed her on his way to the shower.

Knowing her husband well enough after all their years together, Irena recognized immediately that Anatoly had made his decision. She also knew what it was and had to smile.

When the Buskeyevs arrived for breakfast, Abu al Mussari and Qusay Sharaf had tea at the ready. The balcony had been prepared, and everyone was ushered outdoors for breakfast. Mussari avoided the harsh topic of war and weaponry while they dined and deliberately kept the conversation light. They spoke of ordinary things while they ate sweet buttered bread, eggs, and a variety of fruit and cheese while sipping on soft champagne.

As the remains of breakfast were being cleared away, Qusay asked, "I trust everyone was comfortable last night and slept well?"

"Yes, thank you. You have been most congenial; although, giving up the master suite was not necessary, comrade. We would have been just as comfortable in a guest chamber," Anatoly replied.

With reverence, Qusay said, "Nonsense. I would offer nothing but the best for the savior of Iran."

"Please, comrade Qusay, I am willing to help, but I would

never consider myself a savior," Anatoly said, and his voice carried a unique force.

When he heard Anatoly's words, Mussari arose from his chair and exclaimed, "Wonderful! This is a great day." Holding his champagne glass high in the air, he announced, "Here's to a new beginning."

Anatoly echoed the sentiment, raised his glass, and said, "To a new beginning, indeed."

When everyone raised their glass in a toast, Mussari said, "A new beginning, not only for Qusay's Iran, but for Anatoly and Irena as well. Surely, you realize that once the objective has been achieved, you must, for all practical purposes, disappear. Thus, you will be provided with new identities. Your names will be changed and you will have to leave Russia."

Anatoly and Irena nodded, knowing that if any of this information were to be found out, their very existence would be in jeopardy.

After a brief pause, to let his words sink in, Mussari continued his speech. "I cannot impress this strongly enough upon you. Once you have been provided with your new identities, everything you know of the past must be erased completely from your minds. You must never, ever, mention these events to each other let alone anyone else, no matter the circumstances; nor can you ever return to Russia."

Again, Anatoly nodded in agreement while Irena had mixed emotions. She loved her country and had hoped they could enjoy the best of both worlds. But, after realizing the severity of their actions, and if they were ever to be found out, she knew they would be tried as enemies of the state, convicted, and put death. She shuddered at the thought of being whisked away to a top-security prison, not unlike Lubyanka, where prisoners of the KGB were taken, never to be seen again.

"What I said at dinner holds true. You see, I must leave Dubai soon, but before I return to Iran, I will transfer the title of this condominium, along with all it holds, and it will be yours," Qusay said, encompassing the room with a sweep of his hand.

"Now that you have offered your help, and again, Qusay and I give our utmost thanks, I will have the valet gather your belongings and then I will summon the pilot to get the plane ready. We must leave today, as there is no time to waste.

Anatoly found this to be rather abrupt, considering Mussari had shown himself to be a very patient man. Now, suddenly, time was of the essence. Rather than risk upsetting his hosts, he agreed with the plan. He was soon to learn that patience was not one of Mussari's strong points. Finding himself behind schedule was a state Anatoly would find himself in quite regularly in the coming months, only to incur Mussari's vengeful wrath.

On the trip back to Moscow, Irena sat alone near the back of the plane, reading a book, while Anatoly and Mussari were huddled together near the front. The men were discussing tactical matters related to the removal of a nuclear warhead. It was then that Anatoly learned that Mussari wanted more.

"Comrade, I was not aware that you wished to acquire three bombs," Anatoly exclaimed in a hushed voice when he learned that bit of news.

Mussari responded with a quick answer, "What good is one? If Iran is attacked in the city where the bomb resides, then retaliation is futile. It makes sense to have three, each strategically placed, to react in a timely manner. Don't you agree?"

"Hmmm, I suppose that makes sense," Anatoly uttered, his mind in a whirl.

"That will also increase your compensation, if that's what you're concerned with. I believe the agreed to apportion was three million dollars? That was three million per weapon, not three million in total," Mussari reassured curtly.

"No, comrade, it is not the money that concerns me. It is the matter of getting three bombs, not just one, but three, out of the city. One is bad enough. My stress level just increased," Anatoly said with a strained smile as he tried to make light of the situation. The only problem being, he was serious and Mussari knew it.

Having an answer, as he always did, Mussari said, "This won't be as difficult as you may think. I have a contact in the depot. Perhaps you know him. His name is Vladimir Chechenko."

"Yes, I know him. He has worked at the depot for many years. I remember the day I hired him. He's a good man," Anatoly said, and then wondered how long Mussari and Vladimir had had a relationship, and just how "good" a man he really was.

Anatoly's thoughts skipped briefly to the day Vladimir appeared in his office, to explain the reason behind the power outage. He realized at once that the little slip of paper he had found in his pocket, the one containing Mussari's phone number, had to have been placed there by Vladimir.

Keenly aware of his associate's lapse into deep concentration, Mussari left the topic of operatives. He didn't want to be put into a position where he would have to provide details. The less Anatoly knew the better off they would all be.

Mussari worked on a "need to know" basis, and Anatoly didn't need to know much more than this about the people within the organization. He had met too many of them already, just by his reluctance to join the cause.

Mussari continued their conversation by detailing how they were going to achieve their ultimate goal. "As you know, when the USSR was dissolved in 1991, many nuclear weapons remained in Russian territories. They were housed in Belarus, the Ukraine and Kazakhstan, that is, until now. Under the Trilateral Agreement, it had been decided by officials in Belarus, Russia and the United States, that the remaining arsenal would be transferred to Moscow. You, comrade, are in control of upwards of 30,000 warheads."

Correcting the figure, Anatoly said, stoically, "It's closer to 39,000."

"You see? I was correct in my decision to appoint you commander of this operation. Once the depot has been closed down, and the weapons eliminated, you will be far away from a failing Russia, and living a rewarding new life with your wife, in a beautiful and prosperous place."

"I am curious," Anatoly said rubbing his chin. "I would like to know how you propose to get these warheads out of the depot and then into Iran. I'm sure you have it all worked out," he said with a hint of cynicism.

Picking up on the slight, Mussari chose to ignore it, for now. But Anatoly noticed a flash of icy contempt behind Mussari's eyes.

Instead, Mussair provided enough detail so Anatoly would understand his part in the scheme. "Russia is required, by treaty, to destroy a certain number of weapons each year, are they not?" Mussari questioned.

"That is correct," a wary Anatoly agreed.

"Then, you shall process a destruction document for ten tactical nuclear warheads. You will hand carry the paperwork to the special weapons depot in Kazakhstan."

"I am beginning to understand. I will do this as a cover so I can conduct an annual inventory, which is required by regulation," Anatoly added thoughtfully.

"Yes," Mussari replied. "You will be met by the shipping supervisor, a man I have placed there. Together, you will sign the documents reducing the depot's inventory by ten tactical warheads. A copy will be provided for the depot's records. You will hand carry the original, processed paperwork, back to your office. This will be the source document needed to decrease the 'on-hand' inventory of the so-called 'suitcase' weapons on Russia's National Inventory Records."

Thinking through to the end, Anatoly realized an important piece of information was still missing. He said, "I will also need a shipping document prepared for seven tactical nuclear weapons. In actuality, I will be removing seven, including the paperwork, of course, to the Russian Treaty Office Staging Center, outside of Moscow. However, that still leaves the remaining three. How do you propose to move those?"

"I will have papers prepared to ship scientific equipment, three Fluorescence Spectrometers. In actuality, we will be shipping the weapons. They will be packaged in lead-lined wooden crates marked as fragile instruments. But you need not concern yourself with this part of the plan. To ensure these items get to their final destination, someone from my organization will handle it. Once the crates leave your depot, your part in the operation will be over, and you can move on to your new life," Mussari stated quickly, ending the conversation.

What Mussari was unable to tell Anatoly, because he wasn't privy to the information, was that one crate would be shipped overland to Tehran, Iran, where it would be marked for the University of Tehran, Science Department. The other two would also be shipped overland to the Turkish port of Iskenderun. There, the shipment would be met by an operative of Qusay Sharaf. Once they are in his possession, the operative would place both crates into a sea van shipping container manifested for New Orleans, Louisiana, using forged U.S. Air Force Incirlik Transportation Office papers. "U.S. Air Force, Set, Radiology Instrument, 2EA," would be stenciled on the outside of the crates.

When the weapons reach the Port of New Orleans, the sea van would be met by Sanjar Masoumpour, another of Qusay Sharaf's operatives, who would then send them on to their final destinations within the U.S.

· · ·

The voice of the captain came over the speakers alerting the flight attendants to take their seats in preparation of landing. Being pulled out of his reverie, Leonid Karpenko, and his wife, Valeriya, once known as Anatoly and Irena Buskeyev, prepared as well … for the new life awaiting them in Dubai.

Early Spring 1999

A Turkish cargo ship, the Üstünlük, slowly inched into the Port of New Orleans. The seas had been unusually rough during its passage. Sanjar Masoumpour paced nervously as he waited in the hopes that his crate was not among the cargo that, he had been told, had been damaged during the trip. If it was, there would be a long investigation by the insurance carriers, and Sanjar knew his contacts would want to avoid any such delay at all costs. His orders were to destroy the manifest, and then silently disappear, should anything go wrong.

As he waited to take final control of the cargo, Sanjar overheard a conversation between Ralph Johnston, the Harbormaster and Mahmoud Haddad, one of the port dispatchers who also happened to be a Hezbollah operative.

Making an iquiry, Mahmoud said, "I hear there were rough seas."

"Yeah. A lot of cargo on board that ship took on water. I feel sorry for the poor bastards that have to deal with that problem. Looks to me like your freight happened to be on the part of the ship that was spared the worst of it," Ralph said handing a stack of papers to Mahmoud.

"I will still have my clients inspect their loads for any signs of water damage. If they don't, we will be relieved of any further responsibility," Mahmoud answered, knowing Sanjar, for one, would not be interested in an insurance investigation.

With a questioning glance, Ralph looked up at the word Üstünlük painted in bold white letters on the side of the huge vessel, its blue paint faded from years in the sea's harsh environment.

"It means 'Excellence,'" Mahmoud said, reading Ralph's thoughts.

"For you, maybe it does. To me, it means a royal pain in my ass. Looks like I'm gonna be here all night trying to sort this mess out," Ralph responded, shaking his head.

The soggy, well-chewed, end of a burned out cigar hung out of Ralph's mouth. He took off his well-worn New Orleans Saints ball cap and scratched the greasy, scraggly, strands of hair on the top of his balding head. Ralph scrutinized the signature on the paperwork, looked at Mahmoud, and then looked down at the manifest again. Had he been paying attention to Mahmoud's body language, he would have noticed a slight tensing of the muscles and a moment of apprehension as it crossed Mahmoud's face. But times were good, and Ralph had no reason to question anyone employed on his dock. Besides, he had a ton of work awaiting his immediate attention, and this was one less aggravation to deal with.

Ralph turned to Mahmoud, and handed him another stack of copies. Tapping the top sheet, he said, "Scientific equipment, it says there. Better hope the damn thing didn't get wet."

Feeling a moment of unease, Sanjar calmly watched as Mahmoud took the papers, and said, "Yes, that is a fact."

"Well, she's all yours, pal. Have a good day," Ralph said. He then turned his attention to the hustle of activities further down the dock and went in the direction of an unhappy client.

Finally, after a lengthy and uncomfortable wait, Sanjar watched as his sea van was hoisted by a large crane and lowered onto a waiting semi. He would drive to a nondescript warehouse many miles from the port. There, it would be unloaded, away from the watchful eye of the port authority.

Mahmoud handed Sanjar a copy of the documents. The

men's eyes locked for th as they exchanged a knowing look. With a quick handshake, Sanjar climbed into the cab of the eighteen wheeler tractor trailer rig, and drove the long road to an ordinary warehouse located in the small town of Lamar, Arkansas. He didn't have any time to waste as he had important work at hand and, due to the late arrival of the ship, very little time in which to do it.

Many hours later, in the blackness of night, a weary Sanjar arrived at the warehouse. He had hand-picked a few men from his local mosque, men known to be dedicated to the cause. Together, they readied the deadly cargo for its ultimate destination. Once the warheads were uncrated, the men placed each one into a twenty foot, run-of-the-mill, rental truck. The men would travel back roads, avoiding the main highways as much as possible. Their next stop would be the final destination, a place where the weapons would wait for Qusay's next command.

Just before morning light, the trucks drove away from the warehouse. When the vans reached the ramp leading to the highway, they turned in separate directions. One headed east while the other went west. Sanjar watched as they disappeared.

When Sanjar returned to his home, he sent an e-mail to Antesh. The content of the message stated that things were going well in the U.S. and the weather was just as beautiful in the East as it was in the West.

"Babylon is fallen, is fallen, that great city."
—Revelation 14.8

"And slay them (the infidels) wherever you catch them,
and turn them out from where they have
turned you out, for tumult and oppression
are worse than slaughter"
—Quran 2.191

PART II

Canada
Spring 1995

Antesh Moshedian had just returned from a council member's meeting in Iran concerning Danush Enssani and Mansoor Salehain. He sat and watched as the two young men walked, with the rest of the doctorial students, to receive their diplomas. It had taken nine long years of study, but they had finally made it. As it happened, not only were they both scheduled to graduate on the same day, but during the same ceremony as well.

It was the will of Allah.

Of that, Antesh had no doubt.

As Antesh watched the ceremony, his mind drifted back in time to the day he met both young men. They had arrived in Canada, emigrating from Iran, along with their parents and a number of other close-knit refugees. The year was 1977, and the small group had managed to flee just before the Shah had fallen from power. Danush and Mansoor were mere boys when they had arrived in Canada. The Muslim community was intimate, and it was no secret that the boys never felt a sense of belonging in their new homeland. While everyone else had resigned themselves to life in the West, Danush and Mansoor had become increasingly restless choosing to cling to old traditions against the will of their parents. Using that rebellious nature to his advantage, Antesh slowly gained the trust of the two youths who had remained stalwart friends throughout their school years. When they applied to the university, Antesh was able to influence them on a choice of career, so he put them into programs that would ultimately suit the goals set forth by the council.

Both Danush and Mansoor were ideal recruits. All through their years in school they had been honor students, and they both knew that they would never, nor could they ever, accept the Canadian or American societies that they would be subjected to. By the time they had reached college age, they had become completely immersed in the jihadist culture. Since they were Hezbollah, they had been trained to maintain a low profile and above all, how to be patient. They had received green cards and attended citizenship education classes as further demonstration of their desire to become part of the establishment. Antesh considered them to be perfect candidates for insertion into the American sleeper cells. Their behavior and dedication to the cause would be integral to the success of the Hezbollah mission.

With that in mind, Danush had enrolled in Biology, where he received a doctoral degree in Biotechnology, while Mansoor studied Environmental Engineering, also finishing with a doctorate.

During their tenure at school, both Danush and Mansoor had the reputation of being open, friendly, extremely bright and hardworking students. Being their mentor, Antesh took those attributes and developed them into excellent teaching skills, a talent he felt they would need once they graduated and were placed in the field. He had great expectations for them within the Hezbollah organization.

Their exotic good looks made them very popular among the women. Both men were of average height and build, had olive complexions, but Danush had baby blue eyes while Mansoor had curly black hair. They could be found at the most fashionable hangouts with a different beauty on their arm on any given night.

Antesh knew, from the day he had met Danush and Mansoor, both young men would go far in the Iranian Supreme Revolution Council. Because of their intelligence and dedication, it didn't take the young men long to form a solid bond with him. Over time, their devotion to Antesh had become so strong that they both had pledged their allegiance to the cause, and vowed martyrdom should it come to that.

The council had provided Antesh with top secret documents. The papers contained arming instructions. They were provided by Russian operatives, and had been confirmed as the real thing by Hezbollah nuclear experts. The two young recruits were instructed to commit the contents to memory. And they did so, through repetitive study, and this was intertwined with their reading of the Koran. They had proven their excellence

They were also trained to blend into local society. As such, they would not call attention to themselves or to the cause they were fighting. Of all the lessons Antesh provided, the one he impressed upon their young minds the most was, "Always remember to maintain a low profile. Become one of them."

They firmly believed that their part in bringing down the West would be the highest calling one could attain in this life. They were overwhelmed with gratitude that Antesh confided in them. But it wasn't merely confidence that Antesh had shown. They were equally amazed that he would share the council's master plan for North America, and that they had been considered worthy enough to be accepted into a holy mission of such great magnitude and high importance.

If things worked out as planned, and Antesh had no reason to believe it would not, their plan would be the *coup de grâce*, the final step in the beginning of the end of the world in its current state.

The time had come to take it from the infidels … to take it back to the way it was meant to be …

under Islamic rule.

• • •

"Why in the hell hasn't everyone gone home?" Tim cursed under his breath. It had started to rain as he attempted to cross the street, trying to get to his car. It was well past eight and he knew Donna would be angry as a hornet for being late again. Time just seemed to have a way of escaping him. As he jogged across several lanes of heavy traffic, dodging not only raindrops, but vehicles coming at him from both directions, Tim's thoughts returned to the man he had been concentrating his efforts on: Osama bin Laden. He has to be the mastermind behind the most recent terror attacks, not only in the U.S., but around the world. It's gotta be him, he thought.

"If bin Laden isn't the brains, then certainly he's financing the bad guys," Tim had told Stan earlier in the day. But, his accusations were met with admonitions. Stan demanded hard evidence … "Proof!" … and Tim had none. All he had was a hunch; that, and the same gnawing feeling he would get when things were about to deteriorate.

In the settling darkness Tim pulled his car into the driveway, and the first thing he noticed was the house was completely dark, not even the porch light was on. Tim went inside through the garage door entrance, and then scanned the cold, empty kitchen. It was obvious that dinner had not been prepared in their house that day. A note hung on the refrigerator. Tim read it and, with a crumple, threw it in the trash. Donna had taken the afternoon off so she could take the kids to the zoo after school. They were going to stop for a burger and then take in a movie. Knowing he was now on his own for dinner, Tim grabbed a beer, and threw a package of popcorn in the microwave. Carrying his plunder to the den, he sat in his recliner and began his evening ritual of channel surfing. It wasn't long and the kids came bounding through the door, pushing and screaming as each tried to be the first inside. The ruckus didn't end when they finally made it indoors, and the disruption immediately grated on Tim's already raw nerves, the stress from the day taking its usual toll.

With a roar, Tim launched himself out of the recliner and yelled, "That's enough! Go to your rooms, both of you."

Donna had just entered, her arms laden with sacks from a quick visit to the grocery store. Hearing the booming voice of her husband, she said, "Really, is that necessary?"

Taking a couple of the bags from her and then following her into the kitchen, Tim replied, "Damn right it's necessary. They need to learn the proper way to enter the house. They're not a couple of ill-mannered banshees."

Chuckling, Donna answered, "Come on, Dad, they've been out having a good time. You should be pleased that they're happy and pretty well adjusted. Besides, they're just a little wound up. They'll settle down soon enough."

"Damn right they will. That roughhouse stuff is best left outside. I won't have it in my house," Tim insisted with renewed impatience.

"You need to loosen up. They're just kids having a little fun.

You'd do well to try having a little of your own," Donna said annoyed at his attitude.

Turning on his heels, Tim exited the room, but not before saying, "Well, I can see which side you're on."

"It isn't about taking 'sides,'" Donna chided, but Tim was already out of earshot and never heard her sarcastic rebuke.

Tim fell into his chair. He grabbed the remote and began to surf the channels again, not really attuned to what he was viewing, and not particularly interested in anything at the moment. Then, he came across a program that instantly caught his attention. The narrator was stating things that Tim already knew, but he listened intently, anyway.

The Taliban were still waging war in Afghanistan. Since October of 1994 they had captured Kandahar City, along with the surrounding provinces. They were still on the move and since taking Kandahar City, had relieved a war lord of a munitions dump. Tim figured they were on their way to Kabul, Afghanistan's capital. While camera's rolled, showing members of the Taliban flaunting their weapons, the narrator of the news piece continued, "While there is no evidence that the CIA has funded or supported this group of radicals, apparently there has been some military support, along with arms, provided during the 1980s, in an attempt to aid Afghan's bid to resist the Russian threat of invasion."

"Yeah, right," Tim said to the television. "I wonder just how many more billions of dollars we're going to dump into that godforsaken region just so that bin Laden can get his hands on it for the training camps he's set up in the area."

"Who are you talking to, Dad?" Scott asked, taking a seat on the sofa.

"Oh, the stupid news guy on the tube. Do you have any homework, young man?" Tim asked.

"I had a little, but it's done. I had to write a paper on who my hero is," Scott replied, but he looked at the television as he spoke.

Having a feeling he was not the topic of the story, Tim asked, "Do you mind if I ask who you wrote about?"

Stammering and stuttering, Scott tried to dance around the subject when Tim said, "It's okay if you chose someone other than me, kid."

"Well, Dad, I wrote about Coach Patterson."

"That's a great choice, Scott. I'm pleased to hear that you didn't pick someone from a rock band or some other nonsense. Coach Patterson has been around for a long time and I know he's helped you gain confidence through sports," Tim replied with a smile and then turned his attention back to the news report.

Feeling relieved, Scott went back to his room, leaving his father alone again. That would be the extent of their interaction that evening. Tim would not see his daughter, Kristie, until bedtime when she came down to say good night.

Several weeks had passed since Antesh's discussions with members of the Supreme Revolution Council. Finally, after many deliberations and endless conversations, the arrangements had been made. The wheels were turning and the long-awaited plans were finally put into place.

Antesh began by arranging to meet with Danush and Mansoor at an upscale restaurant in the heart of the city. The discussion centered on their future within the organization. Through their many associations, the council had secured teaching positions for the young professors at prominent universities in the United States. Danush would be joining the staff at George Washington University while Mansoor was headed to the University of Nevada, Las Vegas. Going forward, their communications to each other would be limited, and virtually all of their contact would be via the university e-mail system. All messages would be positive in nature and encoded when necessary.

Antesh had also developed a system that was as sinister as it was foolproof. Each man had been handed a slip of paper with the coded instructions. Again, the information was to be committed to memory, the paper destroyed by fire, and the ashes scattered, so that no traces could ever be recovered.

Ensuring that the young professors arrived at their final destinations safely, it was Antesh's task to get them there. With titles and teaching credentials in hand, he could see no reason why there would be any difficulties. Coming and going to the U.S. had never been a problem. Antesh had crossed the boarder many times under the guise of school business, when in reality he was meeting with other members of Hezbollah. No passport was required when crossing into the U.S. from Canada, and no one ever questioned his purpose. He could see no reason for that to change. America, as a country, was wide open. It was a perceived weakness and one they would continue to exploit.

The first trip would be by way of car. Antesh and Danush traveled to Washington, D.C. where Danush spent the next few weeks getting established as a resident. With the help of Antesh, he rented a modest apartment in the affluent area known as Georgetown. Together, they purchased furniture, a vehicle, and then spent the next several days getting Danush acquainted with the area. He had to become familiar with the campus, as well as the clerics in the area mosques. He learned which groups were radical and was instructed to avoid those individuals when assembling his team.

When Antesh felt that Danush had command of the situation, they bid each other farewell. Their contact would be limited, but easily handled with the relatively new cellular phone technology.

The next trip was by air. Antesh and Mansoor arrived in Las Vegas, Nevada, the heart of decadent America. After Mansoor was situated in a house in Henderson, Nevada, Antesh took the same steps as with Danush, getting him familiar with the immediate area, the university, and the clerics who, in Antesh's absence, would take over in the role of adviser.

Antesh was intrigued, as well as appalled, by the debauchery and corruption which he witnessed during his stay in Las Vegas. He had seen advertisements and movies that centered on the city, but now that his conscripts were in position, he felt the need to experience for himself the lifestyle of such a wicked place.

His request to stay was granted, so Antesh bought tickets to a popular stage show. The venue had nude, buxom, women cavorting around the stage wearing nothing more than feathers on their heads, and a G-string with feathers perched precariously upon their behinds. They were supposed to resemble birds, and Antesh was astonished that the audience actually found the content humorous. He found none of it to be amusing. And although he was utterly disgusted by what he witnessed, he was compelled to stay through the end of the show. He reasoned with himself that it was because he needed to give a full account of what he had seen.

The next night, as he walked along the strip, Antesh went into several hotels. The bright lights beckoned to all passers-by to come in and place their bets for a chance to win millions of American dollars. Antesh tried his luck at a few of the games, but quickly learned to quit before losing too much of the council's money.

After just a few days, Antesh had had enough and boarded a plane to return to his home in Canada. He was convinced that the council had been correct in their choice. This was a godless place, the epitome of evil, filled with nothing more than lovers of self and money.

Las Vegas had to go.

• • •

Now that Danush and Mansoor had their teaching assignments, and were settled in their respective environments, they concentrated on becoming part of their individual communities and building their network. In the meantime, they met local girls who found them to be nothing short of fun-loving characters, interesting and charmingly handsome.

But, behind their carefree spirit loomed caged animals, angry and ready to bite the hand of their master. Being ever mindful of their ultimate task—jihad against the West—they would set their sights on a woman with a career, but she also had to be easily manipulated, for they would become unwitting accomplices in their husbands' plans. Each man had instructions of how to go about selecting members of their terror cells and for choosing a mate.

Time would pass quickly.

1997 Autumn
Danush Enssani

Following the words of his mentor, Danush knew it was now time to end the party life and think about settling down. The plan was starting to take shape and Danush had to be prepared once the package had landed in Washington. So, one lazy afternoon in early autumn, while walking in the park, Danush made a point of introducing himself to a young woman whom he had seen around campus. He had watched her movements closely over the past several weeks. She was a rather mousy, reserved, bookwormish sort that never made direct eye contact. Her hair was a dull brown and cut chinlength, and she always walked rather quickly, with her head down, as if searching the ground for some lost bauble. All of her actions led him to believe she deliberately avoided human contact. She appeared to be a loner, just the type of woman that would fit into his world quite nicely.

Approaching the bench where the young woman sat reading, Danush asked, "Do you mind if I sit?"

She looked up at him with an effort and then looked quickly away, her immediate reaction being one of distrust and fear. Without a saying a word she slid down the bench, making ample room for Danush. She then opened her magazine hoping to avoid his gaze.

Easing back against the bench, Danush stretched his arms, yawned and looked up at the sky. He placed one arm on the back of the bench and then, without looking at her, said, "What a glorious day. I just recently moved here from Canada, and they tell me it's already getting cold back home. They say it will be an early winter there."

The young woman continued to read her magazine.

When he didn't receive a response, Danush held his hand out in greeting and said, "Hi. Forgive my poor manners. My name is Danush Enssani. I've just moved here."

Ignoring the outstretched hand, and still looking at the magazine, she replied, "So you said."

With a light, amiable laugh, Danush prodded her on. "Yes, I suppose I did repeat myself. So, do you have a name?"

After a moment's hesitation, "Nora," was the clipped response.

"It's very nice to meet you, Nora …" Danush answered his voice trailing off in expectation of more, but after she did not take the hint, he added, "Is there a last name to accompany Nora?"

Not used to having an attractive man show an interest, Nora was intrigued by his attention. "Yeah, it's Wilcox. So, what sort of name is Danush?" she inquired. Her voice held a hint of sarcasm, and she still did not make eye contact.

Continuing in a voice that was pleasant and calming, Danush answered. "It's Arabic. My family is originally from the Middle East, but immigrated to Canada when I was small. I grew up there mostly, but when I got my degree, I landed a job here. That's how I ended up at the university."

"Oh," was all Nora offered in response, as she continued to try to sound disintrested.

Danush waited for a few moments. Nora fumbled nervously, and while looking away from Danush, mindlessly flipped through the pages of her magazine.

When it was obvious that Nora was not going to interject

further, Danush kept the conversation going. "So, what about you, then? I've seen you around campus. Are you from these parts?"

Nora was taken aback by the fact that Danush had seen her on campus, and then actually remembered her. She was beginning to take a shine to him, and felt surprisingly comfortable in his presence, something she found to be rather unusual considering men typically ignored her, but she kept up her guard. His twinkling blue eyes and athletic physique were hard to resist, so she began to open up just a little. "No, I'm not originally from here. In a way my story is sorta like yours. My dad was in the Army, so my family moved around a lot when I was younger. I've lived a lot of places, so I don't consider myself from any one town in particular."

Wanting to keep her talking, Danush nodded as if he understood the life she had led, feigning interest in anything she may have done.

After studying her fingernails, Nora finally looked him in the eyes and continued, "At one point, after my mom and dad divorced, Mom took the family to Virginia, but we didn't stay. It was a shame because I really liked the area. So, when I graduated from high school, I worked for a while and saved my money. I really wanted to get back here. I eventually did, obviously, and enrolled at GW," Nora said releasing a light-hearted chuckle. She then added, "I don't recall seeing you in any of my classes."

"Well, that may be because I'm not a student. I'm a professor. I teach biotechnology," Danush said with a grin. "Like I mentioned earlier, my work brought me here."

With a slight blush, Nora said, "Oh, yeah, I guess it didn't register. I suppose that may be why I haven't seen you around then. I'm taking general studies with the desire to get into the social sciences or maybe even psychology; nothing as deep as the subject you teach, though."

He finally had her. With an easy laugh Danush added, "Not a problem. Say, can I buy you a latte?"

Taking a moment to consider his invitation, Nora figured it would be okay. He was a teacher, after all, so she answered, "I don't do coffee, but I will take you up on a cup of tea."

"Good. I know of a wonderful little place not far from here that serves a great chi. We can walk or my car is just over there," Danush said, pointing in the direction of his vehicle.

Nora was not sure about getting into a car with a man she had just met. Taken in by his handsome face and alluring blue eyes, and since it was a beautiful autumn afternoon, she opted to walk. So, they went in the direction of the coffee shop. While they walked, Danush quizzed her about her education and started the push towards a degree in the social sciences, a benefit he would be able to draw upon later.

Sitting behind the small table in the café, Danush and Nora traded stories, and he made sure to laugh in all the right places. He prodded and cajoled in the hopes of finding out more about her. He learned that her mother and father were not a major influence in her life, nor did she have any close relatives with whom she kept in contact with. Other than her grandmother who recently died, she didn't seem to be close to any of her kin. From what he could gather, she was on her own. He also learned that she was paying her way through college and didn't own a car. Nora and a couple of her friends were sharing an apartment on the seedier side of town. Danush knew how expensive it was to live in the Washington, D.C. area, so he was not surprised to learn Nora had roommates, but he was prepared to work around that minor inconvenience.

After spending the rest of the afternoon in the little café, Nora accepted the offer of a ride home. Danush now knew where she lived. He asked for her phone number only to learn that the girls couldn't afford a phone. He would have to see about changing that fact as he didn't like surprises and wanted to be able to contact her should the need arise.

Danush put the car into park and let the engine idle. He got out, went around to the passenger door and opened it for Nora. "Thank you for a great afternoon. I enjoyed it immensely," he said, the ever-present charming smile on his face.

"Yeah, me too," Nora said, again averting her eyes.

Taking her chin in his hand, Danush forced her to look at him. With a smile he said, "How about we meet up on campus, say, Tuesday? I have a free afternoon, so how about I buy lunch?"

"Sure," Nora replied nervously. Feeling uncomfortable, she turned to avoid his gaze.

Walking back to the car, Danush called over his shoulder, "I know a great little Italian restaurant, and it's within walking distance of the quad, so if the weather is nice, we won't have to take the car."

Half way in the car, Danush waited for her response before sliding behind the wheel. Nora nodded quickly and then, nearly at a run, dashed into the dingy building disappearing behind the weathered door.

Laughing to himself, Danush thought, Good. Tonight I will call Antesh and fill him in on the details. I believe he will agree that Nora would make the perfect wife.

The sun had begun its slow decent in the west, so Danush pointed the car in the direction of downtown D.C.. He had other business to tend to. With an agenda in mind, he headed to the mosque. There were two men that he believed would fit nicely into the plan. Danush also knew that, through his contacts, he would be able to secure jobs for them at the university. He needed dedicated and committed men in key roles; people who could keep their mouths shut regarding the valuable cargo in their keeping.

Mansoor Salehian

While Danush was busy getting acquainted with Nora, Mansoor had caught the attention of one of the women in the Personnel department at UNLV. She was a striking redhead named Kathy O'Shea. She was a little older than he, but not by much. Unlike Danush, he preferred his female friends to be a bit more outgoing and sociable, while Kathy liked her men with dark hair, dark eyes and an olive complexion. Mansoor fit the bill.

Mansoor had begun stopping by Kathy's office, just to say hello, and as time went on, his visits became more frequent as he worked at gaining her trust. He decided that it was time to end the small talk and learn more about her.

Sitting opposite her desk, Mansoor leaned back in the hard chair trying to get comfortable. Quickly scanning the area he noticed how Kathy had tried to decorate the drab little room in an effort to cheer up the colorless surroundings. Her desk was made of oak, but it had seen better days. The finish had lost its luster and was chipped and pitted here-and-there, but her work area was tidy and well organized. Hanging on the wall, along with a very large colorful calendar, was an assortment of photographs. All the pictures were of the local area and were set in expensive frames. It was obvious that she took great pride in the photographs. Interspersed with the pictures were various pieces of Indian artifacts and fetishes. Missing from the odd assortment of paraphernalia was a picture of a boyfriend or husband.

Noticing his interest in her photography, Kathy said, "In case you're wondering, I took all of those photos."

"Yes, actually, I was wondering. They're very good. So, can I assume, from the number of pictures here, that you like to hike?" Mansoor asked nonchalantly.

"Yes, I do. It's one of my favorite pastimes, well … that and photography. I love the desert," Kathy responded, letting down her guard.

"That's interesting, so do I. In fact, I just put in a request for the position of associate professor at the DEES site."

Looking at the file on her desk, Kathy said, "Yes, I know. I have your application in front of me. It isn't often that a spot comes open out at the Division of Earth and Ecosystem Sciences. It's a popular post." Looking at the papers in front of her, she added, "I must say, you're certainly qualified."

"Are there many other applicants?" Mansoor asked innocently, although he already knew what his chances were. There were always wheels within wheels turning, for him, and Danush, as well. .

"Well, yes, but then again, not really. As you can see, I have a stack of requests, but yours seems to be the only truly qualified one. And I have many recommendation letters on your behalf. But I shouldn't be talking to you about this, should I?" Kathy said, knowing she was speaking out of turn about confidential information. She needed to get her wits back about her, but Mansoor had an easy way and she liked him.

"Don't worry. I won't tell," Mansoor said with a boyish grin, his brown eyes twinkling in good-natured fun. "By the way, I was wondering, how did I manage to be so lucky, you know, arriving about the time a slot came open."

"Oh, well it is a rather bizarre story. The news reported that several of the professors went off into the desert to look for some geodes. It was their hobby. Apparently, one of them had separated from the group and had gotten lost or something. He wandered around without water until he died from overexposure, at least that's what the autopsy revealed. The heat out there is very oppressive in the dead of summer. If you don't keep yourself hydrated, that environment will do strange things to your brain. I always carry a water pack and compass when I know I'm going to be out for an extended period of time. I find it rather odd that he would wander off without water," Kathy mused as she thought about the late professor, an older gentleman, and a man she had known personally and admired.

After a short and somewhat uncomfortable silence, Mansoor walked over to look at one of the pictures. It was a location in the foothills which he immediately recognized. "Since tomorrow is Saturday, how about joining me for an early morning walk along that ridge? We can watch the sun rise over the mountain tops," he said slowly turning his head and looking over his shoulder at her.

Taken by his piercing brown eyes, rugged good looks, and

muscular physique, Kathy relented and agreed to go with him. "On one condition," she added.

"And what would that be?" Mansoor questioned, an eyebrow raised in good-natured fun.

"That we meet at the little café just outside of the campus on Flamingo Road and you let me drive. I know the area like the back of my hand and I won't get us lost. I know how guys are when it comes to asking for directions. Besides, there isn't much out there. You would be hard put to find someone to ask," she added with a pretty smile.

Mansoor wanted to argue the point. He wasn't comfortable letting a woman drive him anywhere, but remembering the words of Antesh, about becoming one of them, he relented. He was determined to get into Kathy's good graces. He decided to wait until morning to argue the point. That's when he would take over and the driving duties would become his. It was a good test; an easy way of finding out if she could be influenced.

The little café was a hotbed of activity, especially during the week, so Mansoor was surprised to find himself the only patron, but it was five o'clock on a Saturday morning. He ordered coffee and cinnamon rolls for two, to go, and waited for Kathy's arrival. He sat near the window overlooking the parking lot and read the morning news. While he waited, a teenager entered the little café. They made brief eye contact, and although he recognized the young man, Mansoor went back to reading the newspaper. Before he knew it, the teen was standing next to him, his hand held out in friendship.

Speaking in hushed tones, and in their native tongue, the

young man said, "Hello professor, my name is Isam Mohammed Hassad. I attend the mosque on Morgan Avenue."

Shaking Isam's hand, Mansoor said, "I am pleased to meet
you, Isam, but please, you don't have to speak Farsi to convince me. I have seen you at the holy place."

Standing tall and looking Mansoor in the eyes, Isam said,
"I would like to become a Mujahedeen in your jihad against
the West.

Returning Isam's gaze, Mansoor asked a serious question.
"What makes you think that I am involved in jihad?"

Continuing in Farsi, Isam said, "I know that it is so. I overheard a conversation between two of the clerics. They did not
know that I was close by. I hate America. I hate the way the
Americans live, but most of all, I hate Las Vegas. I wish I could
leave, but I'm not old enough and my father has grown fat
and lazy. He won't allow me to return to Iran to live with my
uncle."

"I see," Mansoor said, pondering Isam's words. "I will have
to think about it. Now is not the time, and this is not the
place, to have such a conversation. You must go now. I have
important business to deal with today, but I will be in touch."

"There are others that share my feelings," Isam said as he
nodded and walked out the door.

Rounding the corner, Isam's mind was on his conversation
with Mansoor, and was not paying attention. He was nearly
bowled over as Kathy, looking at her watch, quickly made her
way to the entrance. She was running late. She smiled at Isam
and said, "Careful where you walk, young man. I nearly ran
you down."

With a scowl, Isam mumbled, "Sorry."

Climbing into his Jeep, Isam waited for a moment before

leaving the parking lot. He was curious to see if she was the important business Mansoor had to deal with. He watched through the side window, and when it was obvious that Kathy was meeting Mansoor at the café, Isam floored the Jeep, and with screeching tires, entered the highway. He was angry and confused. His mind was reeling. Perhaps they had been wrong about him.

Kathy gave Mansoor a little hug around the neck, and after apologizing for being late, inquired, "One of your students?"

"No, not exactly," Mansoor said, his eyes narrowed as he watched the jeep's tail lights fade into the early morning light. He was concerned about the encounter and knew he would have to seek out Isam, the next time he was at the mosque, to quell any misunderstanding.

Kathy apologized again. "Oh, I'm sorry. I didn't mean to interrupt anything."

"No need to concern yourself with small matters. I am here to meet you, not him. Let's get going. It was my intention to watch the sun come up over the mountain top and if we delay much longer, I'm afraid we will miss our chance," Mansoor said as he ushered her to his car.

Mansoor opened the passenger's door, and just before getting in, Kathy exclaimed, "Hey! I thought I was supposed to be the chauffeur on this little excursion."

Laughing, Mansoor said, "I believe I am quite capable of operating a motor vehicle. If I require directions, I am sure that you, my excellent navigator, will have no problem providing them."

"Oh all right, but let me get my camera and gear before we go," Kathy said with a pout, trying to sound disappointed. In reality, she was looking forward to having the opportunity to enjoy the scenery as a passenger. As the driver she always felt like many photo opportunities had been missed being stuck behind the wheel of a car.

The day passed pleasantly enough, although they did miss the sunrise. Kathy found that to be an excellent chance to, perhaps, repeat the date. "Only the next time I promise not to be late," she said as Mansoor escorted her to the door. Half expecting a kiss, Kathy watched as Mansoor merely helped get the camera gear inside and then bid her good evening.

Later that week, Mansoor went in search of Isam and found him sitting with several other young men at a Muslim civic group meeting. They had just finished prayers and Mansoor presumed that they were discussing the lessons taken from the Koran, interpreted and imparted by their teacher.

"Mind if I take a seat?" Mansoor asked as he sat down between Isam and the other boys on the bench.

Isam excused himself from the conversation he had been having with the group, got up and started to walk away. Mansoor quickly followed, determined to speak with him.

When it was evident that Isam had no intention of acknowledging the request, Mansoor said, "I know you believe that you have a handle on what's going on, but I assure you that you do not."

Isam spun around and with spiteful, angry words, exclaimed, "I saw that American bitch falling all over you and you letting her."

"First off, let me make something completely clear to you, Isam. I don't owe you anything. I have absolutely no reason to come here to speak to you, other than my personal desire to do so. I simply could have let you go on believing whatever it is you want to believe. But, whether you know it or not, I understand how you feel. I know what is going on inside that head of yours, and can relate. Because of those two things, I did seek you out, for I believe you could be of service to my organization."

Angry, confused, and still not convinced, Isam shot back, "What organization?"

Speaking forcibly, but with compassion, Mansoor answered. "I am putting together a group of men who feel as you do … as *I* do. When the time is right, and only then, will we act. But, until that time, we wait and we do what we have to do. If it means using people to meet our objective, then that is what we do. Men and women are our tools and we use them as such; just as the woman you saw me with. It makes no difference, in the eyes of Allah, how we achieve that end."

Calming down and trying to make sense of what he had heard, Isam said, "So, the meeting in the café was a setup?"

"I am not at liberty to discuss my associations, Isam. You must trust that what I do, I am doing at the direction of Allah, for the divine good."

Isam then asked the question Mansoor was hoping to hear. "Do you have a place for me, then, within your organization?"

With a smile, Mansoor said, "I just might be able to use your driving skills."

···

Early Spring 1999

Time marched steadily on. Antesh had sent his regular report to the Supreme council: the ship had landed. The council members received the report with gratitude and responded that they were pleased with the way things had progressed to this point.

Antesh reported that Danush and Mansoor had become entrenched in the American way of life. Even though they despised it, they were living the American dream. Each man had a wife, a nice house, and had started a family. They also had good jobs within the United States university system.

With Danush's help, Nora finished her degree. Through Antesh's influence, and unbeknownst to her, Nora attained an entry level position in the Personnel Department at George Washington University. As far as Antesh was concerned, her new position would be an added benefit. Now he would have even more power over the hiring process at each institution, something he would need to take control of in the months leading up to the prime objective.

Over time, the men continued to be involved with their local mosques. They were directed to avoid the radical, militant factions, in and around their town, for they were surely bugged and under close FBI surveillance. The men were on constant lookout for recruits. They scoured local Muslim civic groups searching for the same sort of resentment they knew so well within themselves. As they found these young men, Danush and Mansoor enlisted them in various activities without informing them of the ultimate plan. The recruits, brainwashed by years of propagandized sermons preaching hatred of the West, followed blindly and willingly. They were pawns and nothing more. But, as Danush and Mansoor knew quite well, once the recruits were "in," they would martyr themselves if called upon. And, since many of the mosques advocated martyrdom as the goal to reap the ultimate, heavenly reward, it was easy enough to find willing advocates, for their desire to martyr themselves was greater than the will of the free man to live.

Danush and Mansoor concentrated on assembling their teams while Antesh focused on hiring material handlers as well as supervisory level positions in the storage and distribution centers at the two universities. When openings had become available Danush and Mansoor used their influence (primarily, with their wives), to get members of their team hired. They knew that these particular men would be responsible for ensuring that the cargo they protected would be kept from prying eyes, and nosey students, without ever questioning what it was they were guarding.

And now, at long last, the time had come to start putting the plan into motion. The bombs had been obtained and were on the move. They had left the warehouse in Kansas and would arrive at their final destinations within days. The cargo had been identified as "Scientific Instrumentation" and marked as Department of Energy Grant Award Equipment, DOE-7900-2008. The bogus documents, supplied by Antesh, and given to the warehouse operatives, were in hand. Each crate would be allocated a spot in the warehouse, specifically used for long lead-time staging, upon the arrival of their respective university's storage center. There they would remain until the orders were given to move them into their final resting place.

The slips of paper containing the code, received by Danush and Mansoor so many months ago, would now be put into use. With the arrival of cellular phones and the popularity of the Internet, every precaution would need to be taken. With that in mind, Antesh had designed his code to be foolproof. When sending information specifically related to the attack, the code word would be "mother-in-law". One would have to understand the code to break the encrypted transmissions.

• • •

Tim Rausch

Tim wondered how much more he could take. The newspaper was full of articles detailing the unrest of various terror groups around the world. He feared for the United States, mainly because of the way the Attorney General was running things. The Wall of Separation, or the Great Wall of Silence, as Tim referred to it, was hampering not only his ability to do his job, but all of his colleagues in the agencies sworn to protect the U.S. That wall was keeping the CIA, his organization, from communicating with the FBI, and vice versa. Therefore, any information that he had on known terrorists, or terror groups, entering the U.S. was relegated to nothing more than a file. He was forbidden to contact anyone outside of the CIA with his information. It took an act of God, or at least a court order, to move forward with any allegation. And as Tim had painfully found in the past, the evidence needed to be pretty concrete for the courts to move.

And then there was the fight for expediency. For many in the CIA, it was easier to give in than to, literally, fight city hall. But for Tim it was stupid simple, and maddening, all at the same time. He felt hogtied and gagged. He knew how effective his operatives could be if they could just team up with the FBI.

And the way the President was behaving, his actions had kept the eyes of the world on his personal life and not on the things that mattered. Things like the 1993 bombing of the World Trade Center and the capture of those responsible.

Tim felt as though he was the only one who gave a damn.

"Stupid simple," he uttered, as his attention turned to the ringing phone.

The concerned voice of his long-time friend, Bob Riszko, met him. "Hey, where you at, Hoss?"

"I'm on my way," Tim responded as he hung up the phone and jumped out of the chair. He picked up his briefcase and dashed out of the door.

"Shit," he mumbled as he ran to his car. Fumbling in his pocket for the keys, Tim looked at his reflection in the car door window, and exclaimed, "Donna's going to be pissed if she doesn't kill you first. You're late for Scott's birthday."

The party was well under way when Tim pulled up in front of the house. He could hear music playing, and the laughter of Scott's friends, coming from the backyard. He had promised to be home on time to cook burgers and dogs for the kids, but he could smell the charcoal and grilling meat when he got out of the car. "Yep, I'm a goner," he said as he put the keys back into his pocket and went inside. He didn't know just how prophetic his words would be.

Krista met him in the kitchen. She had that same sour look Donna always gave him when he didn't perform up to her standards. With her arms crossed firmly against her chest, just like her mother, Krista repeated Donna's earlier sentiment only repeating a phrase more commonly used by Tim. "Mom is really mad at you, Dad. Why do you always do things that piss her off?"

Tim could feel the heat of anger rising under his collar. Trying to maintain his cool in a situation he knew would quickly become heated, he responded slowly and succinctly. "Watch your language. That is no way for a young lady to talk. As for your mother, that is none of your business. We will work it out."

Speaking under her breath and just loud enough for her father to hear, Krista said, "Whatever," and then rolled her eyes and walked away.

Tim responded with anger and yelled, "I'll deal with you later, Krista."

"Whatever," came the screeched response as Krista stomped up the stairs and slammed the bedroom door.

Bob entered the kitchen carrying a platter piled with grilled burgers and hot dogs. Setting them on the counter Bob said, "Donna and JaNelle are outside setting the table. They asked me to cover the plate with foil to keep the meat hot. The boys are finishing a game of tag football and will eat when the game is over."

"Thanks for covering for me. I must have been away from my desk when Donna phoned, but she didn't leave a message,"

Tim replied as a roar from the boys filled the room. Scott had just scored a touchdown.

Just then Donna entered through the patio door, and with sarcastic smile, said, "Excuse me, I did leave a message. Maybe if you would check messages once in awhile, you'd know what's going on at home."

"Of course I check my voice mail. I specifically looked at the light on my phone when Bob called, and it wasn't blinking. To my mind, that means no messages," Tim answered in the same sarcastic tone as he tried to explain.

In an effort to keep an all-out war from developing, Bob interjected, "Okay kids, no fighting. Tim is home, so no harm done. Scott's having such a grand time he probably didn't even notice that his dad was late."

Donna could think of a dozen inappropriate responses, but decided against all of them. She didn't want to put Bob in the middle of her and Tim's issues, so she grabbed the potato salad from the refrigerator, took the platter of meat, and went back out on the deck to finish preparing the table.

Everything okay here?" Bob asked, genuinely concerned.

"Yeah, sure. Why?" Tim asked.

"Oh, I don't know, pal. Maybe it's the way Donna was throwing those daggers at you with her eyes. Or maybe it was the things she didn't say that sort of gives me the impression that there's more to this than just being late for Scotty's birthday. Just a hunch," Bob said as he grabbed a handful of peanuts and popped a few into his mouth.

"Ain't nothing going on here that we can't work through. Don't worry about us, we're fine," Tim said.

"Donna seems to think you're married to the job. Leastwise, that's what she's told JaNelle."

"You know, times are turbulent. There's so much unrest in the world and I know it's heading in our direction. Sure, I spend a lot of time at the office, but it's not like I'm having an affair or anything like that … if that's what your insinuating," Tim said. He opened the refrigerator and searched for a beer. Not finding one, he opted for a cola.

"Hell, I hope I know you better than that," Bob said, and then changed the subject. "So, tell me, does this have anything to do with Hezbollah? Ever since we had that conversation about those guys, I've been hearing their name come up. They've been behind quite a few terror attacks over the past few years."

"Yes, they have. And I'm certain that they have embedded cells here in the US, but because of Reno and that ridiculous Wall of Separation she's put up, I can't communicate with the FBI to share information about some of the bad-asses I have been keeping tabs on. When they drop off my radar, and don't resurface, my gut tells me that they're here, in the States. I have no earthly way of finding out. My own department has me hamstrung, for crissakes."

"Must be frustrating for you," Bob responded with a grunt.

"You're damn right it's frustrating," Tim responded, clearly agitated. Respecting Bob's opinion on a variety of subjects, Tim asked a couple of direct questions. "Tell me, from your perspective, what would happen if we were hit with a ten kiloton nuke? You've already told me how inadequate things are on the healthcare front. Has that changed at all in the months since we last discussed it?"

"Hell no, and to be honest, things are getting worse, not better. Hospitals are terribly understaffed. Some have reduced the number of beds while others have closed down for lack of available funds. In some areas of the country, doctors are leaving in a mass exodus because the local government doesn't have their act together. If a pandemic were to hit, our healthcare system, which I know to be in crisis now, would ultimately crash," Bob responded.

Tim shook his head in disbelief while Bob continued. "But, your question was regarding what the effects would be if we were hit with a nuke, and I'm afraid that scenario is also pretty grim. Do you want a rundown?" Bob asked while the kids partied on.

Tim smiled outwardly at the activity going on around them; the kids playing, laughing and running without a care in the world, yet inwardly, he was concerned about their future. He nodded and said, "Yeah, sure. Shoot."

First of all, our blood supplies are laughable, and we're not facing any sort of dire situation at the moment. But, throw a ten kiloton detonation into the mix, and blood reserves would be totally laughable. That's just for starters. Bring in the burn victims, the people that would require skin grafting. We may as well not even have burn-care treatment because there are only enough supplies for a couple hundred cases, not the massive numbers you would see if there was such an attack. That number would be more like in the hundreds of *thousands*. I'm worried that our ability to perform bone marrow transplants would be woefully insufficient for any sort of a radiological event. But, that's not all, Tim," Bob said, and Tim interrupted.

"Good lord, what else can there possibly be?"

"Our supply chain just cannot support any large scale event that is so supply intensive; for example a nuclear attack or a pandemic. We've gone to a 'just-in-time' inventory replenishing system, joining with the rest of the nation's industries, trying to streamline costs. The problem with that scenario is it keeps no stores on hand for any large scale event that would rely so much on immediate replacement, like a nuke going off or a pandemic. Just-in-time only works for predictable or forecasted demands, which is why it works so well for manufacturing or super markets."

"Great. So, now I'm really depressed," Tim said as he got up to check on the partiers.

Following behind, Bob said, "Hey, you asked."

Approaching Donna from behind, Tim put his arm around her waist. Donna turned with a surprised look, and then with a smile, said, "Burger or dog? Don't wait too long or you won't get any. These kids are eating machines."

"No problem, hon. I can find something inside later. Let them have their fun."

A shout from Scott could be heard above the noise of the music and shouts of the boys, "Hey Dad, we're getting ready to start another game. Want to be on my team?"

Donna gave him a questioning look, but Tim didn't have to think about his response. "Sure kid, but be gentle on the old man," Tim said as he gave Donna a quick kiss on the cheek and ran out to join the game. Bob took his place on the opposing team, joining his son as their wives watched, amused.

• • •

Alexandria, Virginia 2001

Tim entered his apartment and turned on the television.

This had been his home since he and Donna had split. It had been a mutually agreed upon separation, and one that was only supposed to last for a few weeks. It wasn't long after Scott's birthday party that Donna had asked for a little space and Tim agreed, figuring he really didn't have much of a choice. But, weeks had turned into months with no sign of reconciliation. He didn't know if Donna had been seeing anyone since they had been apart, but he didn't think she had. He certainly didn't have the time to invest in another relationship. Tim thought, Hell, I don't have time for this one, so where would I find the time to devote to some strange woman and try to develop some sort of meaningful rapport with her? Not to mention, it was all he could do to squeeze the kids in on the odd weekend, when it was his turn to take them.

Scotty and Krista were angry. They fought against their trips to his apartment. Wanting to be fair, he went along with their wishes, so their visits had become fewer and further between. They always had ample excuses and found their friends to be more important than Dad. Scotty didn't have a problem telling him as much. Tim tried to convince himself that it was normal for kids to behave in such a manner during such trying times, but the truth of the matter was, he felt completely disconnected from his family. Each day that passed, the further away they had become. He knew he had no one but himself to blame.

Spending endless hours at the office had caused a rift in the family unit and that was the breaking point for Donna. She felt Tim was becoming obsessed with work, and his sudden angry outbursts were wearing on everyone's nerves. It had gotten to the point where Donna didn't know what to do. Everyone in the family had become sullen and the kids were tired of walking on eggshells around their dad. Weary of pleading with Tim, without noticeable results, Donna decided that her only recourse was to ask him to leave.

Work had become Tim's number one focus. No … it was more than that. It was his mission in this life to prevent the threat that was facing his country. A danger he knew was coming, but wondered why no one else could see it as clearly as he.

Tim walked over to the safe where he kept his weapons, cash and other valuables, unlocked it, and then removed the topmost journals. He thumbed through the pages, skimming the data, hoping something would jump out at him that would make everything gel. But, it didn't work that way and he knew it. If it had been that simple, everyone would be in agreement regarding the growing insurgency within the boundaries of the United States. Not finding a trigger, Tim placed the journals back inside the vault and turned the combination lock, concealing them once again.

Earlier that day Tim found himself in Stan's office as he tried to get a handle on the pulse of the agency. He was hoping Stan had something to offer. The conversation they had had ran though his mind as he wondered again at the nonchalant attitude of his findings.

"Hey Stan, have you heard anything in the network chatter coming in from the Middle East? I've been talking to the guys again in Near Eastern and South Asia desks, and they tell me that there is a ton of intercepts from Afghanistan, as well as some from the former Soviet satellites."

Sitting comfortably behind his desk, Stan answered, "Yeah, I've heard there is a shit-pot full of messages shooting around the Middle East, Germany and other places in Europe. It's all centered on the same group we've had discussions about before, al-Qaeda. Why?"

"Well, I've lost track of the guy I've been dogging in Russia. The guy's name is Mussari and I know for a fact that he's with Hezbollah. In all the years I've covered this desk, I can't remember a trail going this cold," Tim answered honestly.

Narrowing his eyes, Stan said, "I don't have anything at all on Hezbollah. And I swear to God, Tim, if you start in again with that FBI crosstalk bullshit, I'll throw this damn desk at you."

Knowing that Stan's body language matched his verbal retort, Tim knew the conversation was going nowhere fast. Not wanting to ruffle Stan's feathers, he stated, "That was absolutely not my intention, boss. I was just wondering why the hell all has gone quiet on my front. It really scares the hell out of me."

Feeling a sense of emotional fatigue, he flopped down on the sofa and drifted off to a restless sleep with the last sentence he spoke to Stan echoing in his mind.

The television, a constant companion for Tim when at home, droned on. Now that he was alone, he detested silence and did his best thinking with some sort of commotion in the background which the television provided. At some point in the night, during the telecast of an old war movie, Tim awoke from a horrific dream. When the images finally faded, he realized that the soundtrack from the movie surely caused his nightmare. It had to be the movie and the time he had spent looking through the journals. With that in mind, Tim went to his bedroom to finish out the night. He looked at the clock. It was just past 1:00 a.m.

Tossing from side-to-side, Tim decided to concentrate on

the dream thinking that if he could work it out, he would be able to fall back to sleep. But, the images had faded and the scattered remains vanished like smoke when he tried to put his mind around them. Finally, after several hours of restlessness, exhaustion finally set in, and he drifted back to the distant world of dreams.

The next day dawned sunny and cold. September in Virginia was a beautiful time of year and Tim enjoyed a brisk morning walk taking in the colors of the changing season. The cool undercurrent of the coming season put him in a cheerful spirit.

As Tim worked, his mood remained light. Thoughts of his family came to mind. He called Donna and asked if she and the kids would like to get together that evening for pizza. It would be his treat. He was happy to hear her voice, and pleased when she agreed to meet him at their favorite pizza joint at seven.

Hanging up the phone, Tim looked at the clock. It was time to take a break, so he walked outside to the area set aside for smokers. Although he had kicked the habit, he liked to join in the conversation with those who still smoked.

He casually strolled over to the ash bin that had been provided for the few who broke away from the daily grind for the stress relief of a cigarette. The life of an analyst was not very exciting. Tim found it could be rather monotonous as he spent hours in front of the computer entering data from leads he received from operatives in the field. Out here, with the smokers, he could exchange ideas and pick the brains of some of his colleagues, looking for bits of information he may have overlooked or to merely discuss world events.

Jacob Weinberg was one such individual. He worked in the

Near Eastern and South Asia Analysis group and they always enjoyed a vigorous debate.

"So Jake, what's new in your neck of the woods? Anything you can talk about?" Tim quizzed. Tim was the only one in the agency that got away with calling Jacob, Jake.

Thinking about his answer, Jacob pushed up glasses that had slid down his prominent nose, and replied, "Well, a few things are shaking, but nothing really worth mentioning." Suddenly, his pager buzzed. Tim watched as Jacob's face went pale.

"What's wrong, Jake?" Tim asked with obvious concern, and was immediately met with a chorus of pagers going off simultaneously.

"We're being summoned to the Operations Center. Something is going down in New York. Looks like shit has hit the fan, guys. We had better get going," Jacob responded, as he read the message on his pager, and then scurried away.

Tim, and the rest of the smokers, followed Jacob inside. They assembled in the situation room where they were briefed. Each person in the room sat in shocked amazement as they learned that an aircraft of substantial size had flown into the World Trade Center in New York. They would be brought up-to-speed as more information was made available. They were then excused.

Back at his desk, Tim opened an Internet browser and searched on New York, and selected the news tab. What he saw turned his blood cold. He was met by images of the World Trade Center in flames, black smoke billowing high into the air, and people hanging out of windows, each knowing their chance of rescue had to be slim to none. Reporters were confirming that a hijacked airliner had crashed into Tower One, the North Tower. From what Tim could ascertain, it appeared to be around ninety floors up, too high for normal rescue attempts by the fire department.

Taking advantage of streaming video on the Internet, Tim found a live feed and watched in horror as a second jet slammed into Tower Two. He felt like he had been gut-kicked. His first thought was for the civilians working in the Towers. He wondered briefly if he knew anyone who worked there.

His subsequent reaction was one of anger at his inability to convince anyone in his agency of the threat he knew to be real. Who could have been the perpetrator? The airliner striking Tower Two was obviously a U.S. flag carrier, so could it have been an organization outside of CIA's radar? Clearly, the Wall of Separation had made it impossible to know. But, there was more to come. He, like every other American, was glued to the news. He watched as two other hijacked aircraft left their mark in history as one rammed into the Pentagon and the other into a field in Pennsylvania.

His thoughts returned to that impenetrable wall, set forth by the Justice Department, which prohibited the sharing of information between the CIA and FBI. Frustrated, Tim spoke loudly, and in earnest, to his computer monitor, "See? This is the kind of crap you get when one intelligence agency cannot talk to another. What a *bunch* of horse shit!"

While he pondered the myriad questions running through his mind, an edict came down from the Director. The CIA was on total lock down. The Command Post and Alternative Command Post would be staffed twenty-four hours a day, seven days a week until further notice.

Knowing he was not going to be able to leave the premises,

Tim placed a quick call to Donna. "Have you been watching the news?"

Hearing the grave tone in Tim's voice, Donna replied calmly, "Yes, it's been the main topic of conversation around the office. Our boss has told everyone to go home, but I've been glued to the Internet. This is madness."

Tim's response was brusque, "Madness?" Closing his eyes and rubbing his forehead, he didn't want to take his frustrations out on Donna, so he changed the subject. Speaking in a civilized tone, he added "Well, as you have probably figured out by now, we're on lock-down. I'm afraid I won't be able to meet you guys for dinner. I'm really sorry, Donna," Tim said.

Donna recognized the undercurrent of anger in his voice, and with empathy asked, "Are you going to be okay, Tim?"

"I'll be fine. I'll call you again when I have more to tell you," Tim replied and abruptly hung up the phone.

Setting the handset that had gone silent back into the cradle, Donna muttered, "Same old Tim."

While on lock-down, Tim took the opportunity to review his files. He was interested to know if any of the people he had been tracking, in the Hezbollah organization, had any connection to airplanes, flight training, or flying in general. After several hours of scrutiny, he could not find any links. None of the names on his lists had any interest in aircraft much less using them as weapons.

Later in the day, the Director called a general meeting indicating that the FBI had identified a number of hijackers, and the data indicated that this had been the work of al-Qaeda. Tim was not surprised since Osama bin Laden's name had surfaced many times over the years. What was infuriating to Tim was this could have been circumvented, but had not been due the lack of cross-communication between the CIA, FBI, and other departments dedicated to the defense of the country.

When the director terminated the lock-down, Tim went back to his apartment feeling as ineffective and low as he ever had in his life.

Damascus, Syria
September 15, 2001

Sending a message to its members throughout the world, the leadership of the Supreme Iranian Revolution Council called an emergency meeting to discuss the attack against the United Stated by the terror group, al Qaeda. The reason for the meeting was to discuss the lack of coordination with Hezbollah members in Germany or Saudi Arabia, with regard to their missions.

A furious Sheik Sobhi al-Tofaili faced the group, pointed to a video of a jet aircraft flying into the World Trade Center, and said, "As you can see, al Qaeda has taken the stupid course of action. This will seriously impact our long range goals of taking down America, the Great Satan. These foolish men had zeal, but they lacked brains. Now, we must take very serious measures to keep our agents in America safe and out of the FBI's network. What exactly do we know at this precise moment?"

Responding quickly, and confidently, Antesh Moshedian said, "Our people are safe because they have integrated exceptionally well within their educational institutions and communities in Washington, D.C. and Nevada. They have married, are raising families, and I am pleased to report, they have received their citizenship." Pausing for a moment to watch Sheik al-Tofaili's expression, and watching him nod, Antesh felt it was safe to continue, "These are our best and our brightest. I have spent many years training them, and they are prepared for anything. They know that they must now go dark and lay very low, for at least six months, until we have a better feel for how the Attorney General, Ashcroft, and the FBI will come at the Islamic population. The Bush administration has already determined that this attack is owned by al-Qaeda, and we are hearing stories of a massive retaliation on their strongholds in Afghanistan."

"You are a wonderful planner, and I thank Allah for the day we found you. Take all the precautions you feel are necessary." Sheik al-Tofaili responded.

With his head bowed, Antesh answered, "Thank you for your confidence. I am certain that this has set us back, perhaps years. But, America will continue on its path of Imperialism and, as such, will continue to be a very rich target."

"Very good. Keep us apprised of the situation." With a wave of his hand, Sheik al-Tofaili motioned to his attendants and left the room.

Antesh was relieved to be finished with that meeting.

Two weeks after the attack, Stan summoned Tim into his office for a conversation. Meeting him at the door, Stan said, "Have a seat," and pointed to a chair. He then rounded the corner to take his place behind the desk.

Without uttering a word, Tim sat comfortably and waited.

Stan cut right to the chase saying, "Well, it seems you were right on target about the FBI. The proverbial shit is hitting the fan in Congress and everyone here is scrambling because we are going to get our asses reamed, just like the guys over at the FBI."

Tim couldn't resist taking a swipe at his boss. Responding with a hint of defiance, he said, "We wouldn't be having this problem if that damn wall hadn't been put there in the first place. I was hoping it would come down when Bush got into office."

"You can keep your smart-ass opinion to yourself, Rausch. By the way, I have it on good authority, that it is going to come down now, but of course, it's too late for this catastrophe."

"Sure, too late for this one, but how about getting help from the FBI on my Hezbollah deal?" Tim asked, hoping his past actions would garner some favor.

Letting out a long breath, and biting his tongue, Stan said, "Doubtful. As you know, the hot group now is al-Qaeda. You can bet that Bush is going to kick some serious ass, no holds barred. Look, as far as the administration is concerned, you're taking the ugly girl to the dance. The director is setting up an office on bin Laden and those guys will get the hot babes."

"I don't know, Stan. To my thinking Princess Hezbollah isn't ugly at all. Mark my words, when I get to dance with my girl, she's going to knock 'em dead, no pun intended. I think we're going to find out in the end that she's the Prom Queen," Tim quipped.

"You may be right, but right now my hands are tied," Stan replied, but not nearly as apologetic as Tim had hoped.

Shaking his head in defeat, Tim said, "Just my luck, boss; but I'll tell you now … this attack was pretty bad, the worst ever on American soil, even eclipsing Pearl Harbor, in my mind. But, mark my words, the Hezbollah are the real bad-asses. I'm agonizing over the two Russians that have vanished into thin air, and that Mussari character scares me to death."

"I know how you are. You will dog these guys until you unearth them. Feel free to use any tactic in our arsenal to get a bead on those Russians. Just stay away from the FBI," Stan said reinforcing his stance.

"I figure they're really going to be heading deeper under-ground now with this current event. But, yeah, I'll find them, with or without the FBI," Tim responded with a smile, pleased to hear something positive for a change.

As Tim got up to leave, Stan said, "See you later. Oh, and Tim, on a personal note, I'm sorry to hear that you and Donna are still on the outs. Take some family time, will ya? I'm wor-ried about you."

"Thanks boss, but I'm fine and so is the family." Tim said and closed the door on his way out.

Many months had passed since the September 11 attack. Things were changing at the agency, and getting better, albeit slowly. That fact alone helped Tim's attitude immensely, although he was still very dedicated to finding the missing Russians.

He sat at his desk and pondered his job at the CIA. He knew his overzealousness lead to the decline, and subsequent breakdown, of his marriage. He tried to put a finger on his emotions regarding that fact, but he felt numb to his interper-sonal relationships.

Tim reached for the photo of his family that he kept on his desk. "Geeze, this pictures has got to be two years old or more," he mumbled as he gazed at the smiling faces of his wife and kids. Scott was now taking the separation in stride, keeping busy with friends and sports. Krista was the one he was most concerned with. She had become insolent and very disrespectful to every adult she encountered. Donna was constantly calling with bad news from school and he was the last person Krista would listen to when it came to doling out discipline. He agreed to join the family for counseling sessions, but it seemed that every time one had been scheduled, he had to cancel due to conflicts at work. Consequently, he missed most sessions and Krista's attitude toward him became one of disdain. Donna wouldn't even think about reconciliation at this point because of his record of absenteeism. She had told him that, until he can prove to her that the family was more important than work, he may as well not even think about moving back home. To his mind, he was placing his family above all else, by doing his part in keeping the country safe from terrorist attacks.

Tim returned the picture to its place upon the desk and turned his attention back to work. He had sent out a bulletin, to all the regions within the agency, regarding Anatoly and Irena Buskeyev, hoping someone, somewhere, might have some information on their whereabouts. Folks just don't up and disappear, he thought. Even those with their identities changed could eventually be found.

People slip up. They make mistakes. Of this, Tim had no doubt.

• • •

March 2005

Time marched on. Weeks bled into months and turned into years. Tim, being the man he was, always kept on top of world events and because of his due diligence, had several successful arrests and many attacks that had been thwarted. He always searched for things that might be happening outside of his realm of responsibility, always on the lookout for names and faces of people he might recognize. Anything worth remembering went into his personal data base. He flipped through the pages of the journals, with dates from the past five years, and read through the notes from the events of 2002 that he had found to be of importance.

There had been quite a number of terrorist attacks spanning that particular year, but the most notable one occurred in January. It was the kidnapping and subsequent beheading of *Wall Street Journal* reporter, Daniel Pearl, in Karachi, Pakistan. Even though Tim was most concerned with the Hezbollah or al-Qaeda groups, anything that had an Islamic stamp or involved American casualties made it onto his list. And this attack was both. It was owned by an Islamic separatist organization known as Jaish-e-Muhammad located in Kashmir, and Daniel was an American. Tim shook his head as he recalled the incident. The terrorists had video taped the assassination and sent it to the Pakistani authorities. It eventually made its way to the Internet where millions of people witnessed the terrible and gruesome, act. Four suspects were arrested, and then tried for Daniel's murder. One was sentenced to death while the other three would receive life in prison.

The thing that stood out the most to Tim was the increase in the number of suicide bombings. They were rapidly replacing drive-by shootings and kidnappings. Tim knew how difficult it was to recognize a suicide bomber. They could be anyone walking down the street or standing in a crowd, waiting for a bus or train. He put his hands over his face and wondered how the world had come to be in such a state of abject hatred and intolerance.

Throughout the ensuing months, Bob made sure that Tim's relationship with his children did not suffer from the prolonged separation. Bob was the anchor as Tim's personal ship was adrift at sea. Although, when in public, Donna acted as if there was nothing wrong with their marriage, it was when they were alone that she was distant and detached. Tim always went away feeling worse than ever before. He knew, in the end, they would work things out and reconcile. He wasn't ready to let go of his family, so he continued to let Donna have her space and didn't force any issues.

As for Donna, she was not prepared to go back into a relationship with a man who seemed to be indifferent to the needs of his children and was always on edge. She concluded that life was difficult enough and so decided to go it alone. He knew where they were if he ever made the decision to put them first in his life.

While the rest of the country went about their business, the two professors surfaced briefly, just long enough to e-mail each other. They needed to touch base and felt that sufficient time had elapsed since the attack of September 11. They needed to make much-needed contact.

In a very short message, Danush asked, "Mansoor, my good friend, how are you?"

It didn't take long and a response from Mansoor appeared. "I am doing fine. We just had our second baby, another boy, and he is as strong and healthy as I could have hoped for. My mother-in-law is putting off visiting for now, but eventually, we'll get her to visit. How are things with you?"

Now that the professors had each other's attention, the e-mails were answered straight away. Letting no time lag between messages, Danush answered, "We are doing very well. I have joined a golfing club where some of my friends are taking on the impossible task of teaching me to play the game. Don't worry too much about your mother-in-law, my friend. She will put you in her plans. They always will come to see their grandson."

"Yes, that is a fact, both for your learning the game of golf and the visit of my mother-in-law. How is your family?" Mansoor replied.

"My wife has seen fit to only provide me with daughters. I am disappointed that I have no sons, but my two daughters are healthy and beautiful like their mother. Everything else here is fine. Let me know when your mother-in-law will honor you with a visit," Danush replied.

"That I will most certainly do," Mansoor added, and that was the end of the e-mail trail.

• • •

September 2007

The Hezbollah leadership congregated in Damascus to discuss the final attack upon the U.S.

Sheik Sobhi al-Tofaili took the podium, addressing the group. "We have done extremely well regarding our American planning, and as we had hoped, the Americans are focusing the main body of their intelligence gathering on our cowboy friends, al Qaeda." The Sheik paused for a moment as chuckles went around the room. When the laughter subsided, he continued, "So, dear Antesh, tell us what your final planning consists of."

Standing before the assembled men, Antesh provided details. "Gentlemen, our plan consists of two major parts. The first course of action is to deliver a death blow to the American way of life. The second course of action is to make it impossible for whatever remains of the American leadership, no matter how small, to be able to trace any of our activities to our Iranian heroes and supporters.

"Here is what has already happened. We have two devices, which we obtained from our Russian friends, who are now living in Dubai, stored secretly and securely within the United States. One is at the George Washington University science and technology warehouse where it is thought to be scientific equipment and supposedly awaiting additional pieces to begin working on a Department of Energy Research project. The other is in a similar warehouse at the University of Nevada, Las Vegas. It is also awaits a few more false items to begin work on an Environmental Protection Agency research grant.

"Abu al Mussari is totally faithful and has gone underground.

He has taken a job as a construction laborer in Dubai, and joyously awaits his martyrdom. He is keeping a watchful eye on our Russian collaborators. They are employed by the university in Dubai, where they live a life of bliss as professors. When the event takes place, Abu al Mussari will usher the two Russians to hell on his way to meet Allah. Without the Russians or Abu al Mussari, there will be no connection to Iran. This is a promise that I can make to all."

Sheik al-Tofaili nods in agreement and says, "Please, continue."

"The third weapon is in the most secure area known to us, the Becca Valley. We have also contracted with the North Koreans for their most sophisticated, and dependable, rockets. We stand ready to launch on Tel Aviv," Antesh said and then took his seat among the faithful.

"This plan is the most brilliant I have ever heard. I believe in you, and your ability to plan the most glorious attack in the history of Islam. I will rejoice with Allah in its finality," Sheik al-Tofaili responded.

Silence fell upon the room as the men waited for their leader to continue. After considering the events that had taken place on September 11, and the subsequent governmental retaliations, the Sheik said, "I am a bit concerned about the American intelligence agencies, and their rebuilding under the devil's agent Ashcroft. I am amazed that the FBI has not looked at the universities and their science facilities. Can you tell us why that is, Antesh?"

"Yes. In this case, it turns out that we can thank al Qaeda. Ever since the September attacks, the Americans have exclusively considered al Qaeda their prime source of retribution. They are concentrating on locating and capturing Osama bin

Laden. However, it is my understanding that the CIA is still looking at our operation, but we have frustrated them at every turn."

The Sheik arose as if to speak. Antesh immediately deferred to his superior and moved from the center of the stage to make room for the Sheik, but al-Tofaili adjusted his robes and merely sat back down. When it was obvious that Antesh was confused, the Sheik commented flatly, "I'm sorry for interrupting you, please go on."

Taking a moment to compose himself, Antesh cleared his throat and continued. "Our agents in Washington, D.C., and Las Vegas, Nevada, have done an exemplary job at becoming true Americans. As you know, they have married American women, started families and have become United States citizens. Antesh paused, raised his eyes to the heavens and said, "Allah, please forgive them." Low-key mumbling from the group caused Antesh to pause. When the room quieted, Antesh resumed stating his findings. "The fact is, gentlemen, America has spent billions of dollars fortifying their ports of entry. They are looking exclusively for a threat from outside the U.S." With a dry chuckle, he added, "We could have brought the entire Iranian army through the Port of New Orleans when we brought in our devices. In conclusion, I am pleased to say that we are poised to embark on the final journey. We have made arrangements for our specialist to arm the weapons. The instruction and education will take place very soon under the guise of a Las Vegas Scientific Convention. Once that has been accomplished, we will be at complete readiness to strike whenever you direct." Antesh watched as the men in the room nodded in agreement. Satisfied that there were no questions or comments, he took his seat amongst the rest of the council.

Returning to the podium, Sheik al-Tofaili began his final speech. "And now my friends, let me tell you that I have met with the Supreme Cultural Revolution Council and I have the extraordinary honor to give you the final operational plan of attack. Iran has been building the materials to be able to protect itself from the Jews. There is no doubt in the Supreme Leader's mind that Israel is planning an attack on reactors and other sites within Iran. What the egotistical Jews don't know is that their arrogance will set off the final holocaust not only on themselves, but their American concubines. Iran will keep the pressure on Israel through leaks of Iran's readiness to build a nuclear bomb. When the Israelis can wait no longer, the mother holocaust will begin."

Calls of "Praise Allah," came from the men in the room. The Sheik put his hands in front of his chest, palms out, to quiet the room.

When the men had settled down, Sheik al-Tofaili continued. "Here are your final orders Antesh. When Israel strikes Tehran, launch the first device from the Becca Valley directly on the pigs in Tel Aviv. I will simultaneously release a statement claiming full responsibility for the attack. When that occurs, the Americans will rush into Washington, D.C., to craft their response to this most holy Hezbollah attack. That is when your professors really begin their Islamic duties by demolishing both the center of political injustice, Washington, D.C., and the new Sodom and Gomorrah, Las Vegas. Indeed, what went on there will stay there, resting in a heap of smoldering doom."

Antesh placed a very brief call to Danush. It was time for final preparations.

Danush composed another pleasant e-mail and sent it to Mansoor. "Hello my good friend! My wife informs me that my mother-in-law will be in Las Vegas next week. Since she will be visiting your city during the conference, and I was going to be there anyway, I thought I would bring my family for a visit, too. Perhaps we can meet and break bread together again?"

"That is most excellent news. I will await your arrival. It will be good to see you," Mansoor responded.

The messages were received and acted upon.

The "family" Danush referred to was not his wife and children (although they would be part of the entourage) but the few, trusted, members of the team. They were the men who were most dedicated to the professor, and believed in his cause, even though they had no idea what the cause was.

In Las Vegas, arrangements had been made in advance for the warehouse supervisor, Gahlib Badr, (one of Mansoor's recruits) to ensure the warehouse was prepared for a late night visit. There would be no one but Gahlib on security duty that evening.

The professors met at the conference as prearranged. They participated in many of the meetings during the day and attended banquets with fellow teachers in the evenings. But one night was reserved specifically for them, and using their families as an excuse, they left the world of academia to fulfill the prime objective.

In the darkness, Gahlib led the group to the storage facility on campus, where the weapon had been kept. There, it silently waited in the shadows for the day it would be armed and ready for action. Once inside the warehouse, the professors' instructed their minions to move the crate to a convenient, yet isolated spot, where they could work unimpeded. Danush then instructed the men to stand watch, and sound an alarm, should anyone approach. Danush and Mansoor were then left alone to work.

Quietly, and uninterrupted, they practiced arming the device. The instructions that had been committed to memory years before were easily recollected. After spending several hours working with the bomb, the professors replaced the lid on the crate and then asked the men to put it back in its place within the racks of the facility.

Now that the task of arming the weapon had been accomplished, the professors took a walk along the Vegas strip in search of the most advantageous site for detonation. They took this task upon themselves, leaving nothing to chance. After taking their time and carefully studying the local layout, they finally decided on Tropicana Avenue. They felt that it was the central-most location, and would cause optimum devastation; not only to buildings, but to humans as well. A ten kiloton bomb would not only take out the entire strip, but the heart of the city as well. As they walked, Danush informed Mansoor that the detonation site in Washington, D.C., would be the intersection of Delaware Avenue NE, and Capitol Circle. Mansoor chuckled and said, "I can almost park the truck right in the lobby of the Capitol. There is very little, if any, security around this very important structure."

The use of the Scientific Convention as a cover had been a success. They had mingled with others experts in their particular fields, exchanged humorous anecdotes, and shared laughs, over drinks.

Now that the convention had come to a close, the professors parted company. They hugged each other warmly as they said their final farewell, knowing that it would be the last time they would ever see the other.

Back in their respective environments, Danush and Mansoor maintained their cover by doing all the things a professional would do within their daily routine.

During the final days, as they awaited word on unleashing the holy fire, the professors began a full-court press by educating their followers on more than warehousing and distribution. The young recruits would begin to see the benefits of dedicating their heart and soul to Islam. They were taught about the atrocities visited upon Islam throughout history by the Infidels, and how Muhammad will reward the faithful when their time had come to honor their god. They were true believers and idolized the professors. However, they were never fully apprised of the ultimate plan. What they took away from the instruction was how to follow orders and to do exactly what they were told. In doing so, Allah would be generous in his reward.

When the day arrived, the faithful would not question the orders coming from the back of the truck nor would they question what their professor idol would be doing while en route to the delivery location.

Tim arrived at work at the usual eight o'clock hour. Sitting at his desk he looked at the files that had begun to pile up in his in box. He turned on the computer and immediately received several e-mail messages, but one in particular caught his attention. It was from Jessie Coltrane, an operative located in Dubai. Jessie was an old flame. They had met in college. It was about that time that Tim had proposed to Donna. Relentless in her pursuit, Jessie had even followed Tim into the world of covert operations. When it was obvious that he was going to opt out of field work, Jessie continued on. She had the need for the adrenaline rush associated with being in the field. Tim was content to sit behind a desk and support the field personnel. Over the years, he had remained in limited contact with Jessie, but it had been ages since their last communication, so he was quite pleased to see the new message.

Jessie's cover was as a field architect in an architectural and engineering firm located in Dubai. Reading through her message caused a smile of victory to appear on Tim's face. The e-mail stated that she was responding to his latest call for information. She had found two Russians living a rather luxurious life in a very exclusive condominium in one of the most affluent areas of Dubai. Both were professors at the university, so Jessie couldn't figure how they could afford such an expensive place. Except for their names, Leonid and Valeriya Karpenko, and not Anatoly and Irena Buskeyev as the internal memo had indicated, these two figures matched the profile to a tee. Jessie asked if she should have the condo put under surveillance.

Excited, Tim jumped out of his chair, pumped his fist in the air and shouted, "Yes, damn it! Bug the bitches."

Tim sent a courteous, unassuming, reply in which he asked Jessie to begin surveillance using miniature camera and voice techniques, and to keep a very close eye on them. He then sat back and recalled their early days, together in training. He remembered the affair he and Jessie had had. Tim had already committed himself to Donna, but Jessie had spunk, and a spark that Donna seemed to be lacking. Unfortunately for Jessie, Tim was looking for a down-to-earth woman, someone he could raise a family with. The impression Jessie had given him was one of a free spirit, addicted to living life on the edge, and not the least bit interested in a long-term relationship. He found it ironic that now here he was, separated from Donna, because she couldn't understand the demands of his job. He wondered just how different things might have been had he and Jessie taken that next step. However, he wanted a family and Jessie did not.

The incoming e-mail alert on Tim's computer brought him out of his reverie. Jessie had already sent a response. Sitting forward in his chair, Tim read her message.

"Hello again, Tim. I have sent word to my office to take care of your problem. The surveillance should be in place tomorrow. Our team will enter the premises under the pretext of maintenance workers inspecting the heating and air ducts. Afterward, we will keep a constant watch on your Russians and we'll inform you if we get anything of interest. By the way, how the heck are you? It's been a long time. Take care," and it was signed, "Jess."

Images of Jessie flooded Tim's memory. She had been very lovely back then, with long, silky black hair and a creamy white complexion. She had icy blue eyes that could scare the hell out of you if she was angry or melt your heart when she was feeling amorous, which was quite often. She was also statuesque, a lithe and athletic beauty. He had wondered why a woman of such exquisite femininity would be interested in the life of a spy when she could easily have been a model or an actress. He shook his head at the memory and then composed another benign message. "Hello again to you, Jessie. I'm as fine as can be expected, considering the times. Thanks again for taking the ball and running with it. I have a real bad feeling about those two Russians, and I firmly believe that they will turn out to be the couple I have been searching for. It was great to hear from you. Keep in touch. Tim."

As soon as Tim hit the send button, he wondered if telling Jessie to keep in touch was such a great idea. He felt a little too emotionally weak at the moment and was afraid he would do something he would regret were she to show up now. Even though his kids were rebelling, there was no way he would do anything to destroy his future with them. He and Donna would work things out eventually, of that he had no doubt; but first things first. He had to get through the issues at work. "What good would it do to save my family if the world goes to hell around us?" he asked the indifferent room.

Looking at the clock, and realizing there were still several hours until the end of his shift, Tim felt restless. He put a few files into his briefcase and grabbed his keys.

Leaning back in her chair, Jessie grinned confidently.

Darin Newsome was Jessie's partner, not only in the field as a CIA agent, but also at the architectural firm. Knowing Jessie pretty well, Darin did not miss the little smirk, and asked, "What's that all about?"

"What's 'what' all about?" Jessie asked innocently.

"You know what I'm talking about. That silly little grin you always get when you're up to something."

Laughing, Jessie said, "Lil ol' me? Oh, it was nothing, really. Just a lead I passed on to Langley," Jessie remarked lightheartedly.

"Uh huh, just a lead, and just to Langley. I seem to recall a certain desk jockey who works there that you had the hots for once upon a time," Darin quipped.

"Yeah, once upon a time, a long time ago, just remember that," Jessie responded firmly.

Looking out of the corner of his eye, Darin remarked "You don't know then."

"Know what?" Jessie asked, curiously.

"I hear Tim and Donna have split up. Hell, Jess, he's been living on his own for a couple of years now. Thought you kept on top of things. What sort of a secret agent are you?" Darin asked, poking fun at her.

"I guess a lousy one when it comes to keeping track of old boyfriends," Jessie said, still staring at the words on the monitor.

"Hey, don't give me that line of crap. I saw the look on your face when you sent that last message."

Darin's response was a little too sarcastic and a lot too personal to suit Jessie. Laughing to cover her annoyance, she said. "Well, I never figured Tim and Donna would ever split up. He's too much of a family man … you know the sort, all about the kids. I suppose that's why he and I never made it past casual. I just couldn't do being tied down to babies. Anyway, he's in Langley and I'm in Dubai. That's a bit of a stretch, even for me."

"Still footloose and fancy free, eh Jess? Besides, I think you've both gone beyond the 'having babies' stage by now." Darin said and went back to his office leaving her alone with her thoughts.

Jessie read Tim's message again and her memories drifted back in time as she recalled the torrid affair from their college days. She wondered if he was thinking the same, and if he had changed. Could that flame be rekindled? As much as she hated to admit it, Darin was right. She never had gotten over Tim.

"The one that got away? Maybe not," she whispered and then thought, Well now, we'll just have to keep an eye on those pesky Russians, won't we?

Tim left the office early. He felt like taking a drive to clear his head. As he found himself closer to the D.C. area, he placed a call.

What's up?" Bob asked as he shut the computer down for the day.

"Oh, not much. I was wondering if you had time to join me for a beer."

Looking at his watch, Bob said, "I have a little time this evening, but you know that I don't like to keep the family waiting. I can meet you on this side of town if you want to come this way," Bob responded.

"Yeah, sure. I'm actually not far from your house. I'll meet you at that little bar inside the hotel near the Key Bridge in Arlington," Tim said without a hint of emotion in his voice.

Concerned about Tim's lack of enthusiasm, Bob said, "Hey, man, you okay?"

"Yeah, I'm fine. You know what, on second thought, I think I'll just head back to the house. I don't need to take you from the family. Besides, I have a ton of paperwork that I need to finish. We can have that beer another time."

"You sure?" Bob asked.

"Sure I'm sure; just a little tired. Catch you later," Tim said and hung up the phone. His thoughts of Jessie were best left as that … just thoughts. He didn't need to bring them out into the open.

Turning the car around, Tim went back in the direction of home and a cold supper.

September 2008

Another year had come and gone, and during that time there had not been a single slip-up from the Russian couple. If this happened to be the pair Tim was looking for, they were playing the game extraordinarily well. The conversation coming from their quarters was dull and uninformative, full of boring, intellectual, twaddle. At least, that's how he viewed it. The rest of the time, they talked about their daily affairs. He found it tedious as he read though the daily reports, because they never contained anything remotely of interest, but Tim was diligent. He found it peculiar that they never spoke about nuclear physics while at home, a topic that they had so much in common, and taught at the university. Perhaps it was because they liked to keep work out of their personal lives. Yet he still had a gut feeling that they were the people he had been looking for, and once he snagged them, Abu al Mussari couldn't be far away.

Along with the reports came an occasional message from Jessie. They were full of humor and playful jibes. Same old Jessie, Tim thought. He remained friendly, and they enjoyed the repartee.

The U.S. had not been hit again since the attacks on the World Trade Center in 2001. The current presidency was coming to a close and the elections for a new administration were soon to take place. But for Tim, as it was with every election, he was most concerned about the safety and security of the country. He watched, along with the rest of the world, as the economies around the globe started to erode. Gasoline prices hit an all-time high. The price of staples at the grocery store had skyrocketed while home prices went on the decline.

He didn't know how much more the average citizen could take. There was talk of another great depression as the stock market slipped lower and lower. Retirement accounts began to lose money, and speculation centered on where it would bottom out. But, for all the turmoil going on around him, Tim would cast his vote for the man or woman he thought would see things as he did. The safety and security of the country would have to come first. As long as that was in line, he felt that the rest would fall into place.

But Tim was concerned, nonetheless. He knew the terrorists were watching the way America handled the economic downturn, and were waiting in the wings for the prime moment to strike. The little hairs stood up on the back of his neck when he read an article on the Internet from a freelance writer. The journalist had found an "unnamed" contact, high in the Israeli government, and speaking "off the record," had admitted that Israel was priming the pump, getting ready to "put an end to" the nuclear aspirations of the Iranians. The time had come to end it, once and for all. But, like the terrorists, Tim was patient and waited, knowing that the break he needed would come.

It had taken time, but the break Tim was waiting for finally arrived.

Washington, D.C.
Spring 2010

The sound of the phone interrupted Tim's slumber. He was disoriented and his arms flailed around as he attempted to reach for the phone. But he had fallen asleep on the sofa again, and his phone was not within easy reach. It was still on the dining room table along with his latest journal. He would have to get up to answer it.

Stumbling across the living room, Tim tripped over his tennis shoes and quietly swore as he answered his cell phone. With sleep-laden eyes, he answered without looking at the incoming number. "This is Tim Rausch, and you had better have a damn good reason for calling me at this hour."

"Tim, it's Jacob."

The sound of Jacob's voice got Tim's immediate attention. Now, fully awake, Tim responded, "Jake? Why the hell are you calling me at 0600 hours? Has something happened?"

"Yeah, you could say that. Iran lobbed a nuke into Israel in response to the attacks on nine of their nuclear sites, near Tehran."

"You're shitting me," Tim said sitting down at the table.

"Have you ever known me to be a shitter?" Jacob responded, annoyed.

"No ..." Tim mumbled.

"Israel was prepared for some sort of retaliation, so when the missile was launched, the Israelis blew it out of the sky." After a moment of reflective silence, Jacob added, "I have a real bad feeling about this."

"It ain't good, that's for damn sure. Anyone taking responsibility?" Tim asked.

"Not that I've heard, but I'm already at the office and we're working on it. Thought you would want to know," Jacob said.

"Yeah, thanks, Jake," Tim replied as he hung up the phone knowing he needed to get to the office.

The television was on, but the sound was down, so Tim tuned to a cable channel he knew would have late breaking news. Sure enough, the headline was covering the attack on Israel. As soon word reached news outlets, the buzz was all over American news that Israel had hit nine suspected nuclear sites near Tehran. Yosef Behrman, a journalist in Israel, issued the following report, "A government official, speaking on condition of anonymity, told me that a total of twelve F-16s left Israel early this morning. They flew through Syrian airspace, undetected, by flying below radar reading capabilities. They climbed to 40,000 feet over Iraq and then panned out to hit their intended targets. There were a total of nine nuclear sites in their crosshairs, including reactors and uranium mines."

Tom, the news anchor at the studio in New York, interrupted with a question, "Yosef, you said there were twelve fighters, but only nine sites were targeted. Can you explain?"

"Yes, the remaining three F-16s were there to provide fighter cover for the squadron, and also as back-up bombing support, should that have been necessary. I was also told that all nine sites were either severely damaged or completely destroyed."

"What about the attack against Israel? What can you tell us about that?" Tom asked.

"Iran reacted by launching a nuclear weapon, but Israel was prepared for a counterattack. The incoming missile came from the direction of the Bekka Valley and was intercepted at about 30,000 feet, over Tel Aviv, by one or more of the three Israeli Arrow Interceptor missiles, guided by a new and secret radar system. Israeli Defense Forces were already on high alert expecting some sort of response to its attack on the Iranian nuclear sites. Even though there wasn't a detonation, significant radiation was released over Tel Aviv. As a precaution, the government had thousands of citizens report to hospital to receive Potassium Iodide. They also issued warnings for all to remain indoors and to use their protective masks to insure against radiation entering their lungs."

"Yosef, let me ask you this, how is information getting out to the public?" Tom asked, interested. He knew the U.S. didn't have a way to disseminate important information to the public at large.

"Hot lines have been opened all across Israel, to advise concerned citizens, and to be able to triage potential cases of radiation sickness. You must remember, Tom, Israel lives with the constant threat of attack from many different groups. The people here are prepared for anything."

"Wrapping up the report, it is my understanding that speculation is not how America will react, but how quickly she can get support into the area," Tom said before cutting to a commercial.

Surfing the channels, Tim found another news station that added to the story, stating that the President was currently in Mexico, conferring with authorities, in an ongoing effort to curb narcotics trafficking which had become an ever-increasing threat to the central government of Mexico, its society, and the drug related crimes in the U.S.

Grabbing the trousers that had been thrown on the floor from the night before, Tim listened to yet another reporter as she relayed the same story he had heard on all the other news outlets. His interest piqued when the reporter was told to break away for an important message. The news station had received a video clip from a group claiming responsibility.

As Tim dressed, he watched in anger as the man, covered from head to toe in black robes with only his eyes peeking out from behind a scarf covering his face, and carrying an assault rifle, identified himself as a servant of Allah. He named the Iranian Supreme Cultural Revolution Council as being responsible for the war against the infidels in Israel and the United States.

Tim quickly switched gears and dashed to his bedroom. He grabbed a clean shirt, his shave kit, and then stopped at the kitchen. He threw some assorted canned goods and various other food items into a large backpack because he didn't know when, or if, he would make it home again.

On the way to the office, Tim made a quick call to Donna. When she picked up, he wasted no time in expressing his desire for her to get the kids and get out of town. "Head northwest. Pack just what you need to get by for a couple of days and don't let the kids waste time. You've got to get as far from the D.C. area as you can. I don't think you have much time," Tim insisted.

"Are you out of your mind? I have to get approval to take vacation from work, and the kids are in the middle of exams. I can't just …" but Tim cut her short.

Yelling into the phone, Tim said, "Just do as I say, Donna. Shit is about to hit the fan and I'm afraid something is going to come down, right here in D.C., and I want my family safe! My gut feeling is it's going to be nuclear, just from the things I've been following for the past several years. There was an attack earlier today, against Israel, and that one was nuclear. I just know that the terrorists are going to do something on our soil to keep us from retaliating, and where better than the seat of our government? Our house is too damn close to downtown for me to feel comfortable about you staying there."

Recognizing the fear and urgency in his voice, Donna's reaction was to use the same even tone she always did when he got riled, even though she knew he hated it. It was her way of dealing with Tim's tirades and kept her on an even keel. "Hon, do you really think getting all worked up over this is going to solve anything?"

"Look, you're wasting time bickering about this," Tim snapped. "Get the kids, get some food and clothes together, and please, get on the road before it's too late. Every minute you spend arguing with me is another minute that can be used to get yourselves out of town. Just, please, go Donna. If I'm wrong, then … divorce me," Tim exclaimed, not knowing what else to say.

Taking a moment to consider all Tim had said, and the urgent manner in which he delivered his request, Donna agreed. Besides, she thought, he ought to know. Irritated, she said, "Okay, but if you're wrong, there will be hell to pay."

"There will be hell to pay if I'm right," Tim responded, relieved that she finally relented.

The very thing he had feared was beginning to happen, and he was afraid it was too late to do anything to stop it. He knew that the agency had been focusing on the wrong group of bad guys, and the video from the terrorist confirmed his belief that Hezbollah is, and has been, the real threat. He knew they were already in the U.S., but if he was correct in his assumption, they were in position, and ready to strike. The curtain had already been raised, and they were poised, waiting for the main act. Then, thinking about his friend, he called Bob and delivered the same message.

"Jesus Christ, Tim, do you really think this is it? D-Day all over again?" Bob asked as he looked at his watch, his mind in a whirl as he considered Tim's words, and wondering if he should act upon another man's whim. He knew Tim was usually right, but this really was nothing more than a guess. It would be quite a leap of faith on his part to knee-jerk a reaction and upset his family.

"I don't know, Bob. All I have is a gut feeling telling me that this it. I just wanted to let you know that it might be in your best interest to get your family out of D.C. and head for your vacation home in New York. It took me a minute, but I managed to persuade Donna to take the kids to her sister's place up north."

"What about you? What are you going to do? Stay here and get blown to bits?" Bob asked, still unsure of his next move.

"I'll be staying in my office at Langley. I think it will be safe enough there. It's far enough away from downtown D.C. that I'm not too concerned about my safety, but our homes are too damn close to what I believe is going to be ground zero. So quit wasting time, gather all that is dear to you and get the hell out of Dodge," Tim exclaimed in exasperation as he drove through the early morning traffic, trying to keep his mind focused on two things at once.

"Jesus, Tim, I don't know … but you do sound pretty convinced; that and the fact that Israel had been attacked. It has been percolating for a long time, and everyone knows how closely tied we are to them." After a brief silence, Bob said, "Okay, I'll do it. I just hope you're wrong, pal," and he quickly began getting the wheels in motion to move his family to safety.

"You and me both, pal. Do me a favor and ring me when you're safely outside the city." Feeling like he actually had some control, Tim hung up the phone and hurried into the office.

As word of the attacks between Israel and Iran spread, members of Congress left their homes and office buildings on their way to an emergency Joint Session.

Nearby, a delivery truck with George Washington University Supply Services stenciled on the outside of the trailer, carefully eased out of a loading dock. At the same time, in Las Vegas, the UNLV delivery truck, driven by Isam Mohammed Hassad, began its journey down Tropicana Avenue, assuring their place in history, as well as a ticket to glory.

NEWS FLASH
1:22 PM

We interrupt this telecast to report that we have lost all communication links to our Washington, D.C., Bureau and we have heard from affiliates in Baltimore and Richmond that a massive power outage, and a suspected attack on our Nation's Capitol, has taken place ...

Please, stay tuned.

"And in those days shall men seek death,
and shall not find it; and shall desire to die,
and death shall flee from them."
Revelation 9.6

But those who reject Faith and belie Our Signs,
they shall be companions of the Fire;
they shall abide therein.
Quran 2.39

PART III

Detonation 1:17PM

An electromagnetic pulse had taken down all communications coming in to, and going out of, Washington, D.C. It had also burned out the electronic components of cars, buses, and rail traffic.

A concerned anchor at a major news agency in New York, sat before the cameras and said, "We have lost all contact with our Washington Bureau and have begun receiving reports that all TV and radio transmissions have ceased working." Looking at his co-anchor, and getting shrugged shoulders in response, he read from a sheet of paper that had been handed to him. "Stay with us. We will keep on top of this developing story and provide information as we get it."

In a state of shock, a newsman at a local radio station in Baltimore, Maryland, reported, "Ladies and gentlemen, we have reason to believe that the nation is under attack. We've just received some reports, from several credible sources, that a mushroom cloud has been sighted over Washington, D.C. We also have been told that all traffic has stopped on Interstate 295 and I-395, the two main loops around our Capitol. Wait a second," the announcer stated solemnly, as he paused for a moment to listen to the audio coming in through his headset. Continuing, he said, "I have just learned that all traffic has, indeed, stopped on I-95 as well, heading north and south, near Washington, D.C. Included in the report is that the I-495 Beltway is at a standstill, too. Please stay with me. I will provide all the latest, breaking news."

Other major news outlets also covered the events.

"In addition to the news we have just provided to you, we have also learned, from our affiliate in Reno, Nevada, that Las

Vegas has apparently been attacked with some sort of weapon, perhaps nuclear. We don't have any information yet on the size of the bomb or speculate if this was, indeed, an attack. As you may know, there is a military base just outside of the city, and the reporter who witnessed the scene could have been mistaken." Just as the newscaster was reporting the last piece of information, a frantic producer was instructing him to check his teleprompter. Reading from the screen the news anchor said, "Ladies and gentlemen, we are hearing that virtually all hotels and casinos on the Vegas Strip have been either totally incinerated or are heavily damaged. Please, stay with us as we are receiving updates, literally, as I am reporting this to you." The newscaster put his hand against his ear to be able to hear the reports streaming through his headset. "We are being told that the Department of Defense will be sending information soon and that the DoD leadership is meeting to understand what has happened. Stay tuned, and stay calm, folks."

A message arrived at Unified Command NORAD–US, Northern Command, Peterson Air Force Base, Colorado, known in government channels as NORTHCOM. It was sent by way of emergency transmission.

"This is the watch officer. We have been attacked. I repeat, we have been attacked. It was a ground detonation of a nuclear weapon of unknown yield." The message was sent from the Joint Force Headquarters, National Capital Region, based at Fort McNair, Washington, D.C.

NORTHCOM responded, "Roger that. Detonation detected by sensors. In conjunction with the President, we are placing the United States Armed Forces at DEFCON 2. I repeat, DEFCON 2. Please provide updated situation reports as information becomes available. Over."

The Joint Force Headquarters, National Capital Region, provided their first situation report, also called a SITREP. "Total destruction of all post facilities. Staff of three, in command bunker, only known survivors. All facilities and vehicles lost. We have isolation air systems and are locked down. Will remain on station to communicate future SITREP, sir."

"Roger," NORTHCOM responded.

All the major news sources confirmed, to a nation in shock and utter disbelief, that they have, indeed, lost all communication with the Washington bureau. The United States was under, what they believed to be, a nuclear attack.

At the Pentagon, officials and other staff members that had managed to get inside were assembled in the fallout protected National Military Command Center, also referred to as the war room by the men and women who worked within its hardened walls. The exterior of the building had suffered some minor damage, but the structure remained fully intact. However, radiation readings were extremely high.

The Secretary of Defense addressed the assembled group. "We have been hit with a nuclear weapon, and we are unsure of the delivery vehicle. Thankfully, the President is in San Diego at the Marine base there. He's returning from a meeting in Mexico, and will be boarding Air Force One, not only for his protection, but to assume airborne command and control."

A question came from Marge, a seasoned administrator within the group. "Do we know the status of the first family? They're not with the President, are they?"

The Secretary of Defense answered stoically, "No, they

didn't travel with him, and I was also informed that they are still inside the White House. At this time, I'm afraid we don't have a status on their whereabouts within the building. All we can do is wait for communication and hope that they made it down to the command center in time. If they are there, we will be able to contact them." Turning to Colonel Stanton, the Secretary of Defense issued a command, "Contact the White House and find out the status of the First Family."

With a nod, Colonel Stanton, passed the order down the chain of command and, within seconds, a young sergeant began to hail the White House.

Another message, sent by NORTHCOM, was received at the Pentagon. "Sir, we have detected a second nuclear detonation in Las Vegas, Nevada. It's approximately a ten to fifteen kiloton yield. Devastation is complete on the Las Vegas strip."

The Pentagon responded with an order, "Place radiological response teams on immediate deployment and report to Incident Command staging areas in Philadelphia and Phoenix."

The next message came from the watch officer at Fort McNair. "Damage in D.C.: catastrophic. All radio transmissions from cell towers and satellite media: inoperable. Electromagnetic Pulse damage: widespread, except for a few shielded networks. The EMP wiped out just about everything electronic for miles."

For a moment, total silence enveloped the room as the people taking refuge inside looked at each other. Although highly trained for such a situation, they could not believe what they were hearing, that this scenario was happening and their training would come into play in their own country.

The three men at Northern Command heard a somber

voice as it came over the speaker, "Roger that. Sit tight, men. We appreciate your diligence."

Due to the electromagnetic pulse, traffic in Washington, D.C. had come to a standstill. Vehicles on the interstate systems, in and around D.C., were unable to move. Radiation exposure was extremely high. People in the D.C. area, outside of the blast zone, needed to remain in their homes. But all commercial television and radio transmitters were down, so important public service announcements could not be broadcast. Without receiving the critical information needed to keep themselves and their family safe, local residents wandered outside. Meandering around, they looked dazed and confused.

In Philadelphia, the staff at the Department of Homeland Security had assessed the situation. After several attempts at trying to reach the main office in Washington, D.C., they realized that it must surely have been seriously damaged or destroyed in the blast. Will Hatch, the department head, called an emergency meeting to tell his staff that they must now turn all responsibility over to the military as they have the resources necessary to get into the areas hardest hit.

Recognizing that the survivors closest to the attack zones would be most vulnerable, the Pentagon wasted no time in taking action. Contacting the Department of Homeland Security in Philadelphia and speaking with the utmost urgency, General Morrissey acted upon orders issued by the Secretary of Defense. "We need to start spreading the word, and the only means we have now is by megaphone. Mobilize the information units and get them out now! And make sure the drivers are wearing Level A protective gear. The message to convey to everyone is this. For their own safety, they must stay indoors.

They are to get to the lowest levels within their dwellings. Tell them to seal their doors and windows as best possible. And, for God's sake, tell them to stay put until instructed otherwise!" he commanded.

The Department of Homeland Security immediately responded to the order. "General, this is Will Hatch over at the Department of Homeland Security, Region 3, Philadelphia. As you know, sir, our emergency response capabilities in Washington, D.C., have been lost. DHS is handing off all unified command to NORTHCOM, and surviving senior DHS staff have assembled, either physically or via telecommunications, with NORTHCOM at Peterson Field, Colorado. Most of FEMA command and control functions are now at Mount Weather, Virginia, and backup support is here in Philly. FEMA has notified the Environmental Protection Agency to activate two Radiological Emergency Response Teams. The response teams are being deployed to Philadelphia International Airport, and to Phoenix International Airport, for monitoring D.C., and Las Vegas, respectively.

"Sir, I also want to let you know that calls from the nation's governors began to come in right away after the attacks. They offered assistance in whatever manner necessary. They have National Guard units standing by, as well as civil defense and disaster response teams, at local military bases, staging for deployment. They are prepared to aid in the search and rescue of the folks still in the hot zones and take them to safer areas. For D.C., we'll be sending them north to Baltimore and south to Richmond. As for Nevada, deployment will be north to Ely, and Reno to the west.

"Besides the feet on the street, sir, I have been told that the Red Cross has begun staging blood drives across the country, for there is going to be quite a demand, the likes this country has never seen before."

The General responded, "Thanks, Will. Keep on top of it, and let me know what the flyovers and ground crews tell us. We're counting on you to be our eyes out there."

"Yes, sir," Will replied, in utter disbelief. After all the years he had put in to the safety of the country, both in the military, and then in various roles within the government, he never dreamed it would come to this. After briefing his team, Will considered what he had just done by turning all responsibility over to the Continuity Of Government. Using the COG at Mount Weather was a first. It was an emergency system that had been put into place by President Kennedy, and only to be used in the event of a catastrophic event which rendered the government inoperable. Thankfully, the sitting President was still in charge, but the way the government would run for the next days, weeks, even months, would look completely different. Will's thoughts then turned to the public sector. He wondered how long before the general population would learn of the changes to their way of life, and he wondered, too, just how drastic the changes would be.

All the major cable news networks, still in shock over what was happening, were reporting the same story. All the news outlets in D.C. had been lost and their reporters either killed or were hunkered down in basements of buildings. Those that survived had been subjected to fatal doses of radiation and were not expected to be evacuated in time to be able to save their lives.

A visibly shaken news anchor reported, "All of our D.C. operations have been lost, ladies and gentlemen, along with other news agencies, I'm sure. Please, pause for a moment of silence, and if you're a person of faith, say a prayer for those whose lives were lost today."

Back at the Pentagon, Major Duncan interrupted a conversation taking place between General Morrissey and Colonel Stanford. "Sir, we have contact with Air Force One. The President wants the status of his family in the White House."

Taking control of the conversation, Colonel Stanford said, "Mr. President, this is Colonel Stanford. The First Family is sheltered in the command center of the White House, and all have survived initial detonation."

The President sighed with relief and said, "Thank God."

"However, Mr. President, radiation exposure is unknown at this time. We have DoD data gathering teams, in radiological protective gear, already on the way. We have also scheduled a rescue of your family, and White House senior staff, but we have to wait until the radiation comes down to levels where we can reasonably, and safely, transfer them from the safe room in the White House to the choppers for evacuation," Colonel Stanford added.

"Okay, Colonel. Where will you be sending them?" the President asked.

"To Philadelphia, Sir. We have a command post set up there."

"Very good. For now, if you would, provide an update on the situation as you know it at this time," the President demanded. Colonel Stanford turned the conversation over to the Secretary of Defense who then provided a detailed rundown.

When the Secretary of Defense wrapped up his situation report, the President sat quietly and pondered what he had heard. Finally, after a lengthy silence, the President asked a pointed question. "Do we know if there are any more nukes out there waiting to be detonated?"

"We don't have any reason to believe that there are, sir, but we also have no evidence to the contrary," the Secretary of Defense replied.

When the communication link to Air Force One had closed, the following order was issued by the Secretary of Defense, "All emergency response agencies are to report directly to NORTHCOM designated command posts located at Philadelphia International Airport, Eastern sector, and Phoenix International Airport, Western sector.

Later, on day one, EPA Radiological Emergency Response Teams, or RERT, were deployed, by helicopter, from Philadelphia. The task of taking air samples from Baltimore and Annapolis had begun. After gathering the data from the immediate blast zones, the teams headed southward to all quadrants of Washington, D.C.. From there, they went as far as Northern Virginia collecting samples.

Likewise, other RERT support personnel were in place at Phoenix International where they, too, were deployed. Those teams were sent to collect air samples from Las Vegas, outward, to 100 kilometers. The gathered information would be transmitted to the Pentagon where the data would be compiled, and a situation report readied. Once completed, the report would be sent to NORTHCOM.

A SITREP from the Pentagon was sent to the President aboard Air Force One. The report stated, "At approximately thirteen fifteen hours EST, Washington, D.C., and Las Vegas, Nevada, were attacked. The amount of radiation in both areas suggests the use of nuclear weapons. The details are as follows:

WASHINGTON: Ionizing radiation levels of 5500 REMS near the Capitol indicate ground zero. Status of the surrounding locations: Capitol, leveled; the Senate and House office buildings, leveled; the Library of Congress, all buildings, leveled; the Supreme Court, leveled. The White House sustained major structural damage. The Washington Monument, destroyed. All Cabinet level buildings, destroyed. It is feared that all staff in DHS, FEMA, EPA, the Department of Justice, Departments of Labor and Commerce, and Department of Health and Human Services are lost as well. The only functioning levels of Government, still operational, are those with remote locations and staffed with senior division-level employees. It appears that most Cabinet Secretaries are lost. Civil Support Teams are attempting to evacuate survivors, mostly those in basement locations when the detonation occurred. All surviving personnel will be evacuated as soon as possible and will join the remainder of the U.S. Government at Cheyenne Mountain in Colorado.

LAS VEGAS: Early indicators point to ground zero as the Tropicana Hotel and Casino on Las Vegas Boulevard. The hotel was incinerated. The blast wave and thermal firewall blew out windows and knocked down most of the hotels and casinos all along Las Vegas Boulevard. Everyone on the strip was killed instantly by either: the blast, the thermal fireball, or exposure to dangerously high levels of nuclear radiation. Nellis Air Force Base has, essentially, been destroyed, but the command center is hardened and protected. They are communicating with NORTHCOM, so there are survivors within the facility.

No further detonations detected. End.

The President put the file on his desk and awaited word on the status of his family.

Air Force One landed at Colorado Springs. The President was then taken to the NORAD Command Center to oversee operations.

The Secretary of Defense called a meeting to brief the senior staff. When everyone had assembled, he faced the solemn group and said, "As you know, Washington, D.C., and Las Vegas, Nevada, have been attacked. Someone hit us with nuclear weapons. We are currently evaluating the yields of each weapon, but we estimate the load to be around ten to twelve kiloton. Both detonations have caused catastrophic damage. The Department of Homeland Security has handed off incident command duties to the DoD, and have relocated senior staff to NORTHCOM. Likewise, all emergency response units have been ordered to report directly to NORTHCOM. That is the information we have reported to NORTHCOM, at Peterson AFB, Colorado."

The Secretary paused as he looked at the faces around room. Many had expressions of disbelief, others with questions awaiting answers, while still others had, obviously, been crying. Quite a few of the people sitting before him he had known for years; others he had just met. Clearing his throat, and maintaining a strong demeanor mostly for the sake of the women, the Secretary continued. "On a personal note, I know many of you live within the areas that will be most affected by radiation, and I'm sure you're wondering about your home and your family. All I can say is I'm sorry. This affects me, too. As most of you know, I live in Georgetown. I don't hold much hope of seeing my wife, or my kids, ever again. This may sound cruel and heartless, but I hope that they were taken in the blast and that they won't suffer from a horrendous death caused by radiation sickness. With the electromagnetic pulse from the blast taking out local communications, there's just no way of knowing." Pausing before continuing, the Secretary wondered if the next statement would be true. "Eventually, we will need to prepare to evacuate to NORTHCOM. As radiological symptoms begin to manifest, we will be cared for at the National Hospital. For those of you who don't know, that is the former Fitzsimons Medical Center in Denver.

"But, for now, we are here to do a job. That is our main responsibility, and must be foremost on our minds. It will be difficult, I know. And, it may be a few days before we will be able to leave our posts. Our country needs us. In the days ahead, we must rely on each other for the strength to get through this … for we are Americans and we will get through this!"

• • •

Tim's cell phone rang. Checking the number on the little screen, it identified the caller simply as Bob. Flipping open the cover of the phone, Tim said, "I hope to hell you're well on the road out of town."

"Man-oh-man, I've been listening to the radio reports and when you're right, you're right. Son-of-a-bitch, who would have ever thought the U.S. would take a direct hit like this?" Bob said as he crossed the border into Pennsylvania.

"Where are you right now? Tim asked, hoping his friend and family was well out of fallout range.

"We've just left Maryland and are well on our way into Philadelphia. We're going to keep on keepin' on until we make it into upstate New York. I really hope your terrorists don't choose the Big Apple as a target again, like they did on September 11," Bob remarked.

"I doubt it, Bob. My gut tells me these guys were all about taking out the government, not the financial center," Tim said, but it wasn't reassuring enough to be convincing.

Angrily, Bob said, "Chaos. The bastards want to destroy us from within, by creating mass chaos. Well, they don't know who they're dealing with."

"I don't have time to talk at the moment, Bob. But, stay close to the phone, will you? Right now, I need to contact Donna and the kids, to see how far they have gotten. She said she was taking them to visit her sister. I just want to make sure everyone is safe. I'll be in touch," Tim said, and when Bob agreed, they ended their call.

Immediately, Tim hit the speed dial on the keypad and called Donna's cell phone. It rang several times, making Tim think he was going to end up in voice mail and causing a moment's concern, but Donna eventually picked up.

Knowing Tim would be worried, Donna answered the phone with a statement. "Sorry about taking so long. I'm driving, and my phone was in my purse. Scott had to dig it out for me."

"Thank God. I was getting ready to press the panic button. A thousand terrifying thoughts went through my mind. Is everyone safe? Did you get out before the blast?" Tim asked, the questions pouring out faster than his mind could reason.

"Yes, yes, we're all fine, hon. I told the kids to just grab a few essentials and get in the car. After you called, we were on the road in less than thirty minutes. How bad do you think this is?" Donna asked, afraid of the answer, but needing to know.

"It's bad, Donna. They hit right in the center of D.C. taking out the seat of government, and a second blast took out the strip in Las Vegas. I guess they view Vegas as a place of decadence and excesses, going against their strict value system."

Concerned for her children more than for herself, Donna asked, "Do you think we'll be safe from the fallout?"

"If you've been on the road all of this time, I would think so. You're heading northwest, so the prevailing winds from the blast in D.C. should miss you," Tim said, trying to be as reassuring as he could.

"What about you? Are you far enough away from the blast?" Donna asked.

"I'm at Langley. I'll be okay, just keep your focus on you and the kids and get to your sister's place safely."

Another thought crossed Donna's mind. "What about the winds coming from the West; from Las Vegas?"

"To be honest, I don't know, Donna. Just stay your course, you will be fine. Trust me" Tim said.

With a slight smile on her lips, Donna replied, "I have so far. I don't think I'll change now."

Before ending the call, Tim spoke briefly to Krista and then Scott, telling them both to be brave, be strong, and to help their mother. Times were going to change and their mother would need them now, more than ever.

"When will we see you again, Dad?" Scott asked.

Not having an answer, Tim told him the truth. "I don't know, Son. There's a lot I just don't know right now. But, we will be together again one day, that's a promise."

With renewed determination, Donna pressed on the gas and quickened her pace, resolute in getting to her destination and finding a way to be of service to her country.

• • •

In the months before the attacks on Israel and the U.S., Jessie had requested, and was granted, the use of a microphone and small video recording device to be used in the condo belonging to the Karpenkos. It was placed in the return air duct by two men dressed as maintenance workers. Since that time, Jessie had been watching the couple very closely. She had faith in Tim's abilities as an analyst and figured if the Russians had anything to do with the attacks, and if they were going to slip up, now would be the time.

Today, she was rewarded for her patience. Arturo brought in the daily report as Jessie sat in her office. He said, "Wait until you hear this. I have a feeling it's what you have been waiting for, Jess. Sorry, I don't have any video to accompany it. They weren't close enough to the camera, but the audio is crisp and clear." Handing her a stack of papers, Arturo added, "I printed out a hard copy of the conversation, in case you want to read it."

She opted for the audio version, and read while listening to the conversation, as it had been recorded.

The first voice was that of the female, Valeriya. "Did you hear the news?"

"What news are you referring to, my dear?" the male voice, that of Leonid Karpenko, asked.

Pacing like a caged animal, and accentuating the irritation she felt with her husband, an agitated Valeriya stated, "First, Israel raided Iran by bombing ten of their nuclear facilities. In retaliation, Iran sent a missile, armed with a nuclear warhead, over Israel, which they intercepted and shot down before it could hit the city."

"Yes, I heard the news. How could I not? It was all over the television and radio," Leonid answered calmly.

"But that wasn't the end of it, was it? Later, I learned that two bombs went off in America. One was in Washington, D.C., and the other in Las Vegas, Nevada. That's three nuclear bombs originating out of Iran. Do you think these bombings had anything to do with us, Tolia?" Valeriya asked, quite shaken.

Jessie immediately recognized the use of Tolia. It was a Russian nickname, often used as a term of endearment, and one which Irena had used often when Leonid was known as Anatoly. Jessie continued to listen closely.

Leonid responded without missing a beat. If he had caught the miscue, he never let on or just chose to ignore it. "Of course, it has everything to do with us. We were pawns, nothing more.

I knew from the beginning that we were being used. But due to our circumstances, I refused to see Abu al Mussari for what he was and agreed to go along with his sinister and terrible deception. Now, we have on our conscience, the lives of all those people who have died; not to mention those who are, and will suffer from radiation fallout, in the days and weeks to come."

Jessie made a copy of the recording and put the printed out version in a file folder. Saving both on her computer, she then sent an encrypted message to Tim marked with the highest priority. "You are not going to believe this," she muttered in a singsong voice as she went about her task, and then added, "you are so good."

A Country Changed

A new day dawned on a country forever changed. The Commanding General at NORTHCOM agreed to a press conference. Not having slept the entire night, General Ted Anderson reviewed his notes for the meeting set for 0800 hours.

Sitting over a cup of coffee, General Anderson talked with General Eugene Clayton, his chief of staff. "Tell me Gene, how does one inform the American public that their country has been attacked from within? We were caught completely unprepared."

"I don't know, Ted. I'm still trying to come to grips with this myself," General Clayton responded.

"Hells bells," General Anderson sighed, and then looked at his watch. "I guess I had better get going. The press is waiting for answers. I wish there was better information to pass along. I know many folks out there had friends and family in D.C. and Vegas," General Anderson added, his voice sounding tired and empty.

"This is one briefing I don't envy," General Clayton said.

The men walked together in silence to the briefing room. General Anderson took his place at the podium, facing the cameras. He put his notes down and waited for his queue, while General Clayton took a seat behind him.

Looking around the room, General Anderson noticed a sea of emotions on the faces of the reporters. He and the press never could see eye-to-eye. He was a staunch conservative and they had labeled him a war monger because he never hesitated to suggest the use of military force as a means to curb aggression against the United States or her allies. Today, he hoped they would understand why men like him existed. The room was extremely quiet, but he knew, after the briefing, it would come alive with questions, and he would have few answers.

General Anderson was given the sign that the cameras were rolling, so he stepped up to the microphone and began to speak. "Ladies and Gentlemen, yesterday we were attacked with two nuclear weapons, each with an estimated yield of ten to fifteen kilotons. They were aimed at destroying our seat of government, as well as Las Vegas, Nevada, which appears to be construed by our enemies as an insult to Islamic sensitivities. Due to the recent bombing in Israel, we believe these two attacks were perpetrated to keep the U.S. from retaliating against those responsible for the act of aggression against our ally.

"For those who may be wondering, the President is secure and leading America from the temporary Presidential Office at NORAD headquarters in Cheyenne Mountain.

"This is what we have for you this morning, but please be advised that this situation is very fluid and the information is as accurate as possible in this turbulent environment."

Taking a pair of glasses out of his coat pocket, General Anderson adjusted the pages in front of him and began to read the statistics. "Ladies and gentlemen, as a result of the worst attack in American history, most of our federal government has been destroyed and, with that, the vast majority of federal officials and employees working in our Nation's Capital. In Washington, D.C., the loss of life and property can only be characterized as profound and catastrophic. Suffice it to say, the buildings in the Mall area are either obliterated or have been damaged beyond repair. As for the loss of life, these are our best estimates on the distribution of casualties: approximately 50,000 dead on the scene. We estimate another ten to 20,000 with blast injuries, and another 150,000 with second and third degree burns. In the hours and days to come, we anticipate about 50,000 individuals will develop severe radiation sickness, and approximately three hundred thousand more will suffer moderate radiation sickness. Those who have been exposed, but are not expected to have any clinical manifestation of illness, three to three point two million in the Washington metro area.

"In Las Vegas, Nevada, due to the nature of the population, we approximate 100,000 dead on the scene from a combination of structural collapse and/or thermal radiation, or the hot fireball. Blast injuries are unknown, again, due to the fluctuation of the population on a daily basis. Estimates for second and third degree burns range from fifteen to 20,000, and as many as 50,000 with severe radiation sickness. Those with moderate radiation sickness will be in the range of 100,000, while those who have been exposed, but are not expected to have any clinical manifestation of illness, 900,000 in Las Vegas and surrounding areas.

"We have mobilized CSTs or Civil Support Teams, and the Marine chemical-biological incident report force, known as CBIRF teams. We have also called upon special radiological monitoring teams to go into the hot zones. They will be equipped with FOX radiological sampling vehicles from various DoD and National Guard units. Currently, they are en route to Philadelphia International Airport. They will conduct search and rescue operations in what is still a very dangerous radiological environment. BWI and Reagan airports are closed to all air traffic and will remain so for some time to come."

Taking a moment to scan the pages of notes in front of him General Anderson continued, "Last evening DoD Civil Support Teams, outfitted in level A personal protective equipment, which is the highest level of protective gear that we have, rescued the first family and all the senior White House staff. They were transferred by military Chinook helicopter to Philadelphia International Airport. Upon arrival, they were transferred to a Veterans Affairs hospital in Denver. Some of you may know this facility as the Fitzsimons Army Medical Center. In the meantime, by order of the President, the Veterans Affairs patients have been relocated throughout the VA Integrated Service Network to make room for the incoming casualties. The Medical Center will now be designated The National Medical Center. In addition, Public Health Service Commissioned Officers have been deployed to the National Medical Center to care for federal officials, and others, that have survived the nuclear attack on Washington, D.C..

"The President has recently joined his family at the hospital and is extremely grateful to those who went the extra mile, at their own peril, to rescue his family and staff and he wanted to me express his utmost thanks.

"As for the hospitals in the Washington, D.C. area, all have sustained severe structural damage from the original air blast. The patients and staff have been profoundly affected by the thermal radiation, as well as exposure to extremely high doses of ionized radiation."

Concluding his briefing, General Anderson said, "I will take your questions now."

The room came alive with reporters scrambling to be first.

General Anderson randomly pointed and the room quieted as he received the first question.

"General, do we have an idea of what the death toll is at this point?" the young man from the Washington Post asked.

Looking through his notes, General Anderson replied, "Current estimates have that number at around two hundred thousand to three hundred thousand causalities. Keep in mind the exact number of casualties and fatalities won't be known for weeks or maybe months since we can't get any rescue personnel in there. All we have at this time is our properly protected Civil Response Teams and that is a limited number of personnel. This will be the most catastrophic attack in America's history."

Someone from the back of the room shouted, "General, what about the patient load at the hospitals?"

General Anderson turned to Major Cecilia Evans, a ranking officer in the Marine Medical Corps, and one of the few still alive in the immediate D.C. area, and said, "I am going to turn that question over to you, Major Evans."

Stepping up to the podium, Major Evans responded bluntly. "The Air Force Medical Evacuation group, in St. Louis, has sent air evacuation planes to Philadelphia, but most of the casualties are either still in the hot zone awaiting rescue, or are not stable enough even for air evacuation. Hospitals in Bethesda and Rockville, Maryland, as well as Northern Virginia, Annapolis and Baltimore, are totally overwhelmed by people who have somehow self-transported and presented with burns, blindness and extreme symptoms of gastrointestinal bleeding.

"All reporting hospitals are requesting medical supplies of every type, especially burn and wound dressings, IV fluids, ventilators, and enormous quantities of morphine and other pain medications. Virtually all hospitals have locked down. Some medical staff, emergency medical services, and many volunteer physicians, nurses and others, have been treating patients in the parking lots and in areas adjacent to emergency room entrances to care for all of the sick that are showing up and in need of immediate care. And that's just Washington, D.C.

"The major hotels and casinos on Las Vegas Boulevard, once known as the Strip, have been either totally destroyed or have been extensively damaged. National Guard units from Nevada, California, Arizona, and other nearby states, have deployed Civil Support Teams. They are currently conducting search and rescue operations on the Strip and in other locations in the greater Las Vegas area.

"Since all the Las Vegas hospitals are either destroyed or overwhelmed with casualties, most of the survivors have self-transported to Reno area hospitals. And similar to D.C., they are urgently calling for medical supplies and radiation antidotes. All the area hospitals are out of burn and wound dressings, as well as morphine and other potent pain killers.

"I repeated that last statement, about the need for pain medication and supplies, because you need to fully understand the severity of the situation. Requests have gone out for massive quantities of burn and wound dressings, and almost every category of pharmaceuticals and radiological antidotes. It translates to literally thousands of line items just for medical goods that we have requested from our allies. Our National Medical Distributors are unable to come even close to supplying the demand for medical items of this magnitude. This has become a worldwide support mission of unprecedented scope."

A seasoned reporter from a major television news station stated, "So, what you're saying, Major, is that our hospital systems and emergency management agencies were caught off guard. This is just the beginning of a horrible death for thousands of people who will not be able to be cared for properly. Ma'am, literally thousands of people are dying as we speak. There won't be any pain medication to ease their passing,"

General Anderson approached the podium again, made eye contact with the reporter and merely nodded his head. Then in the hushed stillness of the room, he said, "Son, I served in Vietnam and both Gulf Wars. This event will require many times the medical support than all of those wars combined. What's more, it will threaten the continued existence of our country and its entire population. However, efforts are underway to reconstitute our federal government, and with the help of all Americans we will prevail as a people."

Hands went into the air and shouts of "General" or "Sir" filled the room before the next question was asked. "Sir, can you comment about the direction of the prevailing winds and the effects the radiation will have on those populations downwind?"

"That's a good question, and one I asked as well. I have been told by experts in the field that, in Washington, the winds were from the west-northwest, eventually ending out over the Atlantic Ocean. Unfortunately, there are large populations in the path of those winds. Those populations will be affected by fallout.

"In Las Vegas, the winds were from the west, heading due east. As for the populations in both of those areas, the numbers of those potentially affected were included in the statistics provided earlier in the brief."

More shouts from the reporters as the next question was raised, "Sir, do you know who is responsible for these attacks and where they got their nukes?"

"I'm sure you have all seen the video from the group identifying themselves the Supreme Cultural Revolution Council. They took responsibility for the bombing of Israel. Although we have not received a similar video for these attacks, we believe it was the same group due to the timing of the detonations here. However, we have no concrete evidence at this time that it was that terror organization, but our intelligence agencies are working around the clock to find the people responsible to bring them to justice," General Anderson responded, hoping that would be the final word on it. He wouldn't be so lucky.

"Do you think the President will respond with a nuke of his own?"

That question, was fired immediately and with a very condescending attitude, by Ken, a young journalist and one of the most liberal in the media. Ken was very outspoken about the use of force and then only as a last resort and in extreme circumstances. Even in light of the recent attacks, he felt that communication, and trying to reason with an adversary, was always the better way to approach a conflict.

The General wanted to tell Ken that he wouldn't hesitate blowing the bloody bastards to smithereens, and likewise, couldn't comprehend anyone not being in complete agreement. But in this situation, he knew best how to respond. "I'm sure that once the President has all the data and intelligence on the matter, he will weigh all options and do what's in the best interest of the country."

"What about you, General? Would you lob a nuke?" Ken asked in a very degrading manner. The room became unnervingly silent.

Knowing Ken was merely trying to get his goat, General Anderson remained cool. In a steady, even voice, he leaned into the podium, and said, "It appears to me that you aren't getting it, Ken. This attack is the worst thing that has ever happened in our country's history. When it's all said and done, hundreds of thousands of Americans are going to die a horrible and painful death. God forbid that it is someone in your family or a friend or a neighbor. However, it is up to the President to determine what our response will be. Right now, there are tens of thousands of Americans dead, dying, or being exposed to massive levels of radiation. I recommend you get your act together and stop grandstanding or think about reevaluating your career choice."

On that note, General Anderson ended the news briefing by thanking everyone for attending, and then exited the room.

Walking together down the corridor, General Clayton said, "I think that went pretty well, Ted, considering."

"I don't know about you, Gene, but I think those folks are in for a rude awakening. They've never seen anything like what they are about to witness when they reach ground zero. Even though the devastation on nine eleven was terrible, it will pale in comparison. The hell of it is, I know they're chomping at the bit to get out there, and for the life of me, I can't figure out why."

With a shrug of his shoulders, General Clayton responded simply, "All for the love of the story, Ted."

"Well, that's the last place on earth I'd want to be, but I have no choice. I have to go. I'll be leaving when the chopper gets here," General Anderson replied, and then left to prepare for the trip.

Dressed in a Level A protection suit, General Anderson took his first look at ground zero. He had a pretty good idea of what to expect, but was still shocked at what he saw, never believing he would actually see his nation's capital completely obliterated. The Capitol. The seat of government for the greatest country on the planet, the place other nation's feared yet respected … destroyed. All gone. Idiots, he thought. You merely took out a place, not an ideal. We're still here and you will rue the day you took us on.

It was deathly still and eerily quiet. There was not a sound from machine, man or beast. Every building in the surrounding area had been knocked down or was completely incinerated. As the General moved away from what was perceived to be ground zero, he started to come upon bodies scattered about. And then, at about three blocks from his starting point, burnt hulks of bodies were everywhere. Not one tree was left standing as far as the eye could see. They must have been vaporized along with everything else, he surmised.

The General had to blink a few times to make sure that what he was witnessing truly was reality. The place he had known, like the back of his hand, was completely unrecognizable now. Picking his way through the rubble, General Anderson tried to get a bearing on where he was and how things were supposed to look. As he carefully made his way around the ruins of what was once the Mall he could find nothing identifiable. Chunks of marble and shards of glass crunched under foot as he slowly walked along. In the distance, fires still burned and smoke filled the skies. He also knew that, eventually, he would come upon wounded, the burned and dying. They would be the people who had worked in what was once a vibrant city. Further out, away from the hottest areas of the blast, others would be succumbing to a slow and agonizing death from radiation poisoning. It would be days before a full-blown rescue could commence.

Moving further outward, away from the center of the blast zone, General Anderson called his team together, gave them their orders and then left them to do their work. He had seen enough and was ready to report his findings.

The President demanded information, but more to the point, he wanted answers. So his instructions to NORTHCOM had been to provide, at a minimum, hourly updates, even if there was nothing new to report.

The chopper landed, returning General Anderson to the command center at NORTHCOM. After removing his protective clothing, he placed a call directly to the President. "Sir, I have just returned from a firsthand look at the Capitol, and the devastation is worse than any of the images I have seen from the bombings of Hiroshima and Nagasaki. Just about every structure from the Capitol to the White House to the Library of Congress has been either damaged or destroyed. Fires are burning all around the perimeter of the blast zone, and the smoke is thick enough to cut with a knife. If there is any life at all out there, God help them."

"Understood. General, how long do you think it will take before D.C. will be inhabitable again?" the President asked.

"Well, sir, from what I know about nuclear radiation, it won't be; at least not for a very long time. I also believe the psychological scars associated with this attack will make it a very undesirable place to be; probably for generations to come … if ever. If I may, Mr. President, you will have to designate another city as the Nation's Capitol."

The President spoke with quiet firmness. "I'm well aware of that. However, for the time being, government will have to be run from Cheyenne Mountain. Even though things have been quiet for a couple of days, I want to be certain that there won't be any more bombs going off. Finding another Capitol is not high on the list of priorities at the moment."

A myriad of responses, none of which were appropriate, ran through General Anderson's mind, but he maintained his military discipline, and answered accordingly, "Yes, sir."

"Okay, that's Washington. Tell me about Las Vegas."

"Personally, I have not seen it, but the reports and images coming in from ground zero are quite disturbing. The level of destruction appears to be far worse due to the makeup of the area. There was limited radiological protection because the hotels were constructed mostly of glass, not granite or cement. That's why there was a much higher death toll initially. Again, the fire storm caused perimeter fires which have been compounded by explosions from furnaces and stoves in local homes and office buildings. That residual event is happening in both locations, in the areas just outside of the blast zone. Due to the nature of the poisoned atmosphere, getting the fires under control is difficult. It's going to take a lot of manpower, in the right environmental gear, and there's just not enough of either at both locals right now. I've been told that governors from across the country are offering to send help, but it takes time to get the trucks, men and equipment where it needs to be, sir, but we're working on it. Getting help to the population that's still alive will be our number one priority."

With unmistakable frustration in his voice, the President said, "Who is responsible for this? I want to know what country or radical group is taking ownership."

"We're not sure, sir, but we have people working 'round the clock. We have some leads that are very credible and promising," General Anderson replied.

"Good. Brief me when you have more. I want every little piece of information you uncover, no matter how insignificant you think it may be," the President demanded.

Without warning, the President ended the call. Sitting with the handset still in his fist, General Anderson wanted to throw it across the room, but deep down, he knew it was due to exhaustion. He figured that the President was just as angry as he, and probably just as tired.

Tim awoke with a stiff neck. He had fallen asleep at his desk. He had no intention of going home. Things were happening now that he didn't want to miss. Rubbing the back of his neck, he powered up the computer that had gone into sleep mode, along with him, hours before. When it had booted up, he checked the clock. It was well past eight and he needed to wash the sleep off his face and try to find something to eat. He was starved. He walked down the hall to the men's room amid a bustle of activity and chatter from the other analysts and agents on site. He listened as best he could to what had transpired over night. From what he could discern, no other bombs had gone off, but he felt confident there would not be any. He walked down to the cafeteria, but there was no one in the kitchen and the vending machines were empty.

Back in his office, Tim used the key which opened the

large file drawer in his desk. He kept it secured because today it contained items worth their weight in gold. It had only been a matter of days since the bombs had been detonated and already food had become a scarce commodity and getting it, difficult. Fearing that another attack might be immanent, people were stripping grocery shelves of anything and everything they could get their hands on. The hoarding mentality had taken over. In much the same fashion as when the weatherman forecasted blizzard conditions, the masses were stocking up on food, water and anything else they felt to be a necessity. Except, unlike the weather, this raid upon the grocery stores was occurring after the fact, and supply lines were quickly drying up.

Opening a large file drawer, Tim scanned the contents. This was where he had stashed the food and water he had brought from home. There were small containers of hot cocoa, tea, instant coffee, crackers and peanut butter. There were various canned goods consisting of soup, meats and fruit which he had added to the stock of MRE, Meals Ready to Eat, which he had purchased from the local Army/Navy surplus store and kept on hand.

Placing a tea bag into the hot water he brought back from the cafeteria, Tim checked his e-mail. Munching on a cracker, he read the first message that caught his eye. It was highlighted in red, contained attachments, and was flagged "urgent." It was from Jessie.

Wasting no time, Tim opened the e-mail and read the contents which simply stated, "You are so good." There were two files attached to the message. Not knowing what to expect, he clicked on the audible, and listened as Anatoly and Irena discussed the bombings in Israel and the U.S. He didn't quite know how to feel about the revelation other than vindicated, but that was hollow at best. As he listened to the conversation, he printed out the hard copy transcript, which Jessie had always supplied, intending to take it to Stan.

This was the break they had been waiting for, and desperately needed.

Back in Dubai, Jessie had provided the details of the dialogue to Darin. After several phone calls to Langley, it had been decided that Jessie needed to get to Virginia immediately. The information she and Tim had been tracking would be of the utmost interest to the President.

"I'll get your flight arrangements made. You go on home and pack a few things," Darin urged.

"Thanks Darin. This is tragic, and it makes me so damned mad! If they would have just listened to Tim, this might have been avoided," Jessie said as she gathered her purse and jacket.

"Maybe, maybe not. There's just no way of knowing these things. You'll make yourself crazy if you try to reason it out," Darin said, knowing exactly how she was feeling. Then, trying to lighten the moment, and with a wink, Darin added, "And don't forget to take that sexy little black strapless number with you, because you just never know."

Thinking about Darin's comment, Jessie countered, "You know, I doubt there will be very much to celebrate. I'm looking forward to seeing Tim again, but would rather it be under much different circumstances."

"Yeah, I guess you're right. I was just trying to add a little humor to a sad situation," Darin said apologetically.

With a sweet smile, Jessie said, "I appreciate it."

Meanwhile, Abu al Mussari decided to pay a visit to the

Russians. The time had come for the last part of his mission and his glorious entry into Allah's kingdom.

Leonid was surprised to see the scruffy construction worker standing at his door, but upon further scrutiny, he recognized the eyes peering at him from behind the sun-dried face. "Abu al Mussari," Leonid exclaimed. "Please, come in," he said as he opened the door for his old comrade.

"Thank you. I don't plan to stay long. I just wanted to see how you and Valeriya were doing. How do you like Dubai?" Mussari asked politely.

Joining the group, Valeriya said, "Dubai has been quite an experience. The work at university has been very rewarding, Comrade Mussari. It's very good to see you again."

Lying, Mussari said, "And you as well. As you can see, I have also been living in Dubai, and working various construction jobs. It was time for me to leave my previous employ and I had always enjoyed Dubai. So, I found a rather simple line of work. No stress."

"Please excuse our inhospitality. Could I offer you something to drink? Or perhaps you would like to join us for dinner. It would be lovely to be able to repay you for the kindness you had shown to us," Valeriya said hoping he would decline the offer.

"Thank you that would be very generous, but just a glass of something cold would be fine," Mussari responded following the couple into the sitting room. Getting comfortable on the divan, he took the drink offered and continued, "I am pleased to see that you have enjoyed the time spent here, as I have. Dubai is a wonderful city, don't you agree?"

Leonid and Valeriya nodded in unison. They were wary and not sure what to expect from Mussari's visit.

As he watched his audience, Abu al Mussari could tell they were uncomfortable. By that fact alone, his task would be made easier. He said, "I can also tell that you have enjoyed the hospitality of Qusay. This condominium is still as pristine as the day you moved in."

"Yes, and we only had one small problem with heat and air maintenance since we have moved in," Leonid countered.

A look of surprise came across Mussari's face, one that was real and not put on for show. He was truly shocked and said, "Please, tell me more."

"We received a call some months ago about a problem with the air ducts. The management told us that two maintenance workers would come in and test the air to make sure it was safe. There was some concern over carbon monoxide getting into some of the units. Of course, we complied because carbon monoxide is deadly," Valeriya said.

This was just the opening Mussari needed to get the pair out of the house. "I am afraid your safety has been compromised, comrades. Please, come with me. I will take you to a place where you can hide, unobserved, until which time it will be safe to move you to another location."

"Should we pack?" Valeriya asked as Mussari arose and hastily made his way to the door.

"No, there is no time. I must get you out of here before they come for you. There will be everything you need where we are going," Mussari responded.

Mussari was convinced, beyond a reasonable doubt, that the condo had been under surveillance and the council's anonymity may very well be compromised, as well as his own. There was only one course of action and it had to be now. Quickly leaving the confines of the condominium, the Karpenkos', once again blindly followed Mussari.

The trio drove out of the city and that would be the last anyone would see or hear of Abu al Mussari and the Karpenkos.

. . .

Stan scratched his head. He had just hung up the phone from a conversation with Andrew Winton, the director of counterintelligence at the agency. From what Stan could gather, some interesting intelligence had come in from Dubai; information that had confirmed what Tim had been saying for years. Hezbollah was the group they should have been concentrating on all along. Now, it appeared, the President wanted to be briefed on what the CIA knows. Tim would be the perfect person for the job, and he told Andrew as much. Not surprisingly, Andrew now wanted to speak to Tim. Just as Stan was prepared to contact Tim, the light on his phone lit up.

"Yeah, Tim, I was just about to ask you to come to my office. I have some news that might be of interest to you," Stan said.

"Really? Could it have anything to do with Hezbollah?" Tim asked innocently knowing the information he had surely made it to Stan's office.

"Don't be a smart ass. Just get down here," Stan snapped. He was in no mood for an attitude.

Moments later, Tim found himself in his usual seat across the desk from Stan. Getting comfortable, Tim waited and was quickly rewarded.

"I just got off the phone with Andrew Winton," Stan said bluntly.

Trying not to read too much into Stan's attitude, Tim remained calm. Andrew Winton doesn't call just to shoot the breeze. Even though is mind raced, Tim kept a level head and his mouth shut. His flip comment on the phone was not received well, and he knew better than to press his luck, especially when Stan had just spoken with Andrew and was in one of his moods.

"Yeah, seems you've had a bead on the bad guys all along, Tim. Apparently, one of our agents in Dubai forwarded some Intel on those two Russians you've been hunting for the past few years. It appears they have popped up as professors at the university in Dubai."

"I received that same bit of information myself. In fact, I had just finished reading through the report. I was going to come and see you when you buzzed me," Tim said placing the printout on Stan's desk. He knew things were about to get interesting.

"Andrew has sent for Jessica Coltrane, the agent that had their condo under surveillance. She'll get here tomorrow, and he wants to meet with both of you. I want you to have all your ducks in a row when the two of you meet with him. We need to get this right. I told him that, without a doubt, I believed this to be a Hezbollah attack, and that you may have the missing link to Iran." Stan said, a hint of a smile breaking the corner of his mouth.

"I'm on it," Tim replied.

As Tim walked back to his office his thoughts were scattered. He had talked to Donna the night before. She and the kids were safe and secure at her sister's place in Winnebago, Wisconsin. Donna said she was thankful that he had made them leave, even though she had been convinced that he had been overreacting as usual. The house they had shared, for so many years, was in an area that would have been hard hit by fallout. At this moment, there was no telling if Donna and the kids would have been victims or not. Donna was making overtures of finally becoming a family again. And Krista, who would always be his little girl, was becoming a young woman and growing as an individual. The last time they had talked, Krista had mentioned how much she missed him. She didn't care for Winnebago and was looking forward to coming home …

… and now this.

Jessie boarded the plane bound for Philadelphia and then a short ride, on an Army helicopter, into Langley. As she sat looking out the window of the CIA jet, her mind searched for the connection to her heart and she began to ask herself some tough questions. What exactly was she expecting out of this reunion with Tim? Deep down, Jessie knew that Tim was all about family … his family. Thoughts of their early days together, when Tim was torn between having a relationship with her, or moving on and settling down with Donna, entered her mind. The mere fact that he had chosen Donna spoke volumes about the sort of man he was. The fact that he was still married, even after so many years of separation, was also a telltale sign. He wasn't ready to let go. Reaching deeper into her emotions, she wondered if she really expected that of him. What's more, did she want him to, especially since America has just experienced the worst attack imaginable? His family would need him now and he would need them. Sure, she would give anything to be the one he told, as they turned out the lights for the night, that everything would be okay.

No, Jessie thought. Not now, and not like this.

Tim deliberately refrained from meeting Jessie's helicopter at the heliport; however, he could have easily persuaded himself to do so. Instead, he called Donna to see how she and the kids were doing.

"We're okay. It doesn't look like we will be coming back any time in the very near future. I've actually been asked to manage a site where people can come by to donate blood. It gives me a chance to use my skills as a phlebotomist," Donna said.

"I thought you hated that line of work," Tim said jokingly.

Surprised by his reaction, Donna tried to defend herself. "I never hated it, I just didn't feel it paid enough for what we needed at the time."

"I know, hon. I was joking. I'm proud of you and what you're doing there in Winnebago. Things are really pretty bad down here in D.C.," Tim responded wearily.

"I can't imagine what it's like and forgive me for not wanting to know. But I figured that it has to be pretty bad. They have us gathering platelets, whole blood, packed cells and plasma, among other things, so it has got to be just horrible," Donna reiterated. "They say there will be more people needing transfusions, in the days to come, than we will be able to supply. How can that be?" she asked, finding it difficult to comprehend.

"Because no one expected that something like this could ever happen here. Therefore, we didn't have the protocols in place to respond in a reasonable manner. We were caught with our pants, not only down, but way down around our ankles. We were simply unprepared for something as devastating as this."

After a brief silence, Tim thought about telling Donna about Jessie's arrival, but decided against it for the time being.

Things were going pretty well and he didn't want to rock the boat. After all, he could see no reason for anything to happen with Jessie. It had been a long time.

Finally, after listening to silence long enough, Donna said, "Okay, I know you're busy, and you sound dreadfully tired. I'll let you go. I hope your getting enough rest and not sleeping at your desk."

"I am and I'm not," Tim said with a yawn. "I'll call again real soon, okay?"

Donna chuckled in spite of herself and then said, "Okay," and hung up the phone.

Tim wanted to concentrate on reviewing his notes in preparation for the teleconference with the President. But now, here he was, at headquarters, face-to-face with Jessie. She was sitting across from him at his desk, sharing an intimate breakfast of potted meat, crackers and hot tea, all of which had been taken from his personal cache.

Listening to Jessie as she recounted her trip to the states, Tim remembered why he had been attracted to her so many years ago. Even in these trying times, she exuded a zest for life that was contagious, and her beauty had not diminished over the years. He had to smile as she described, in detail, her encounters at the airport. Without intending to, Jessie had a way of turning an ordinary story into a Keystone Cops style adventure. Add in her flamboyant arm waving and exaggerated facial expressions, she could easily have been a stand-up comedian.

Continuing to take command of the conversation, Jessie's demeanor became serious again as she turned to the reason she was in Langley. "I take it you've had a chance to review the material I sent."

"Yes, absolutely. And without a doubt, these two are my Russians, Anatoly and Irena Buskeyev."

Reaching into her briefcase, Jessie removed a large envelope and set it on the table. "Here, take a look at these and tell me if you recognize anyone."

Tim reached across the table to pick up the envelope and, as he did so, brushed her hand. "Oh, sorry," he said, with a red face, and was surprised at his emotional reaction.

"Are you sorry because you touched my hand or sorry because you're blushing?" Jessie asked with a devilish grin.

Tim decided to let the question ride and removed the photos from the safety of the packet. But if this was the Jessie he knew from days long past, then the question will come up again. In the meantime, they had work to do, so he let it ride.

As Tim scrutinized the first photograph, he immediately recognized Anatoly. Thumbing through the remaining pictures, he also noticed a figure in the background in many of the shots. The man was slightly built, had a full, dark beard, and wore sunglasses. In one photo, he carried a shovel, and in another he pushed a wheelbarrow. But, the thing that Tim immediately recognized in each photograph was that the man was looking in Anatoly's direction, and if not for the sunglasses, Tim figured he was looking dead on at Anatoly.

With a nod, Tim handed all but one of the pictures to Jessie, and said, "Yep, that's Anatoly Buskeyev. I have no doubt in my mind ... that's him."

"He's also known as Leonid Karpenko. The woman is his wife, Valeriya, or Irena, as you know her," Jessie responded.

Taking the photo that was still in his hand, and pointing to the man in the background, Tim asked, "Who is that guy? He looks vaguely familiar to me, like I ought to know who he is. He also appears to be conveniently hanging around in a bunch of the photos."

"Boy, you are good," Jessie said with a smile. Reaching into her briefcase she removed another envelope. Handing it to him, she said, "Here. I figured you would sniff him out."

Tim slid the sheet out of the envelope. The face looking back at him was a computerized rendition of that same man, only without the beard and sunglasses. "I'll be damned. Abu al Mussari," Tim exclaimed. "I thought I recognized that slimy bastard! I always figured that when I found the Buskeyevs, he wouldn't be too far away. I never figured he would put himself in such close proximity."

"Well, you have to admit, his disguise was pretty good. You didn't know who it was," Jessie said teasingly.

With a short grunt, Tim said, "Maybe not at first, but I would have puzzled it out; probably in my sleep. I get a lot of epiphanies that way."

"It took us some time to figure it out, too, and we were not nearly as quick to notice him in all the photos. The guy has some cojones, I must admit," Jessie said as she put the pictures back into the envelope. When the pictures were back in place, she added, "You're not going to believe what else Darin and I uncovered while we were watching the Buskeyevs."

Just as Jessie was about to provide additional details, Tim's cell phone beeped an alert. "It's a text from Stan. He wants us to come to his office. had sent a text message asking him and Jessie to get to his office right away.

Stan handed Tim a printout. It was a message he had received from the office in Dubai. Tim couldn't believe what he was reading and with a shake of his head, handed the memo to Jessie.

"Looks like your boys dropped the ball on this one," Stan said, the barb being directed at Jessie.

"I don't know how they could have let a thing like this happen. Before I left I gave explicit instructions not to let the Karpenkos out of sight, that they were crucial to our investigation," Jessie said, exasperated.

"I have a sneaking suspicion that this man, ushering them into a conveniently waiting vehicle, was none other than Abu al Mussari. Unfortunately, the picture is not very clear, but I'd bet my last buck that's him," Tim said pointing to the blurred image on the photograph that Stan had just printed. "Can you have the lab try to clean this up?" Tim asked.

"No need. Mussari showed up unexpectedly at the Karpenkos' flat. From the audio retrieved earlier, he surmised that they were being watched and offered to take them to a place of safety. My guess is all three are long gone, and if I had to stake my job on it, they're probably dead. Mussari, tying up the loose ends by blowing the Karpenkos, and himself, to smithereens, all for his share of the virgins," Stan replied, sitting down at his desk.

"Yeah, well I hope the virgins are all men," Tim added sarcastically. When Stan looked at him sideways, Tim added with a shrug, "Where does it say that the virgins had to be women?"

Jessie stifled a laugh, took the photo and scrutinized it. Handing it back, she said, "I have some other information that might be of interest, and I was just about to tell Tim when you asked us to come to your office. When we learned that the missile that hit Tel Aviv came from the Bekka Valley, we checked with the guys handling Korea, and sure enough, they

— 211 —

found a link to a sale of a Taepodong-2 missile. It was sold to the Iranians within the past few months. They're sure of it, due to the fact that the sale was made to a man who claimed to be weapons intermediary known for his connections to Iran. The only group allowed to authorize the sort of purchase would be the Supreme Cultural Revolution Council."

"The same bunch taking credit for the bombing of Israel," Tim said, stating the obvious.

With a nod of her head, Jessie said, "We learned this tidbit just before I left Dubai."

"That seals it. We now have the missing link connecting Mussari, the Russians, Koreans, and Iranians, to the attacks against us and Israel," Stan said, satisfied that they could now go to the President with solid facts.

• • •

The days passed slowly as Americans waited, along with the rest of the world, for some sort of answer as to what happened. The press were out in force and had converged on the areas hardest hit, but were not allowed into D.C. or Las Vegas proper due to the dangerous levels of radiation. However, there were a few journalists allowed to be embedded with Civil Support and CBIRF teams.

Reporters, with their camera crews and satellite trucks, arrived from the New York bureaus, their affiliates tagging along in support. They positioned themselves in casualty staging areas in Rockville, Silver Spring, and Bethesda, Maryland, and in various areas in the suburbs of Arlington, Virginia. Some had even managed to acquire some level of protective gear, in the hopes that they could persuade someone in authority to let them be one of the first on the scene. Reporters stopped and asked questions of anyone that looked to have some authority only to be disappointed by getting a vague, non-response, or worse, brushed-off.

The central meeting point was a small airport in Baltimore, but they were not allowed to venture out. A few tried, but much to their dismay were caught and sent back. The military had the airport cordoned off in such a manner that it was just about impossible to try to sneak around them. Closer in to D.C., the roadways were still blocked by stalled vehicles, forcing the media that did manage to sneak out, back to their starting point.

Los Angeles and Phoenix affiliates congregated in Reno, Nevada, to cover the events in Las Vegas. As with Baltimore, authorities would not let anyone past their checkpoint due to the amounts of radiation still in the area.

Although the journalists wanted to be on scene, they had no idea what horrors were waiting.

The airwaves across America, or what used to be America, were saturated with nonstop coverage of the mass destruction which had taken place in both cities. Tony, a roving reporter said, "In my twenty years of covering news events from around the world, this is, by far, the worst I have ever witnessed. Flying in, I could see cars stopped all along the interstate systems which surround the city, not to mention other roadways in and around the D.C. area. I'm not sure I want to know what it's really like on the ground. It's reminiscent of a scene out of Dante's Inferno; just horrendous."

Don, the news anchor, covering the story from the studio, asked, "What can you tell us of the situation in D.C., Tony?"

"The military won't let us get close to D.C., but I still can't believe what I am seeing here in Bethesda. It's like a flood, only this flood is people. I can't get my head around this either. Isn't this supposed to be America?" Choking back tears, Tony continued as best he could. "I see people, hundreds of them, with skin falling off, screaming in agony. I've never heard anything like that before. It's like they're already dead and their souls are screaming. I'm not sure if I can handle this, Don. I was in Vietnam as a reporter and these poor souls, being evacuated and brought here to Bethesda, are far worse. At the very least, and at the worst of times, we had Morphine in Nam. These folks are dying in torment. I'm not going to last long here."

The airwaves went silent for a moment as Don waited for Tony to compose himself. When he felt he could continue, Tony said, "In answer to your question, I'm afraid I don't have anything on center city D.C. right now. We flew in by chopper and landed at the airport in Baltimore, and then came out to an evacuation staging area here in Bethesda. Even the few taxis that are around were afraid to come any closer to D.C. than this. Anyway, aircraft have been ordered to keep away from ground zero, so I can't even get a bird's eye view, had I wanted to. Only the military and a few rescue teams are being allowed in for now. If the amount of stalled vehicles on the roadways is any indication, there's going to be a lot of folks getting real sick real soon," Tony answered with dismay.

"Radiation sickness," Don stated bluntly.

"You got that right, and it makes me wonder where all the sick people are going to go. It's obvious, from what I have seen here early on, that we, as a country, just were not prepared for something of this magnitude," Tony said with conviction.

Likewise, coverage of Las Vegas echoed the sentiments of

the reporters covering the demise of D.C.. They were a discouraged lot, but eagerly anticipated the word that they could go in, as each wanted to get the scoop on the other. The correspondents in Reno were reporting very similar findings regarding people with burns and various other wounds. However, all pain medicine stocks had been completely exhausted on the first wave of evacuees.

An on-the-scene reporter, Jane Kilpatrick, faced the camera. Ashen-faced and looking ill, she said, "I have never seen anything like this. Nurses are crying in anger and frustration because they can't help the influx of people that are pouring in. They have nothing to work with. All the hospitals in the surrounding areas are overwhelmed, the caregivers are overworked. People are dying in agony and in numbers I have never thought possible. Doctors are yelling at Civil Support Teams to bring in medical supplies immediately. I've been told that they are out of burn dressings, pain medicines and IV fluids.

"I'll tell you this, I have never seen nurses more distraught. I was in New York on September 11 and it was nothing at all like this." Jane heaved once, put her hand over her mouth and briefly left the scene. When she returned, her face was more ashen than before, and it was apparent that she was struggling with the human element of the story. Continuing her report, she said, "I will never get over these sights. This is just horrible. I have seen babies and small children with their clothes literally burned into their skin. They are hoarse from crying because there isn't anything to help them with the pain and suffering they are experiencing. Some patients have lost their entire face. I couldn't tell where their eyes and mouths were supposed to be. For lack of a reasonable description, it was like looking at burnt hamburger. People are sick with extreme internal bleeding, and they have lost bowel and bladder control. There is blood everywhere, mixed in with vomit and excrement. The smell is indescribable. And the voices of the dying … it's just unfathomable. There is nothing to help ease their passing." With tears streaming down her face, and no longer able to maintain composure, Jane said, "Back to you," as she quickly disappeared into the news truck.

And reports from around the country were echoing the same sentiments. Sheldon Wood, another news anchor at a major news outlet said, "We are in contact with several of our affiliate stations around the hardest hit areas. Sally Spiers, are you there?"

An attractive young, reporter was standing outside a treatment center in Northern Virginia. She was holding a handkerchief over her nose waiting for the cue from the cameraman. When she lowered the hankie it was obvious that she, too, had been crying. Turning her tear-streaked face to the camera, Sally spoke, trying her best to hold back the tears. "Yes, I'm here."

"What can you tell us about the scene there in Virginia?"

"I cannot begin to describe the horrors that I have witnessed here, Sheldon." As Sally spoke, the cameraman panned the room. "As you can see, there are patients everywhere in excruciating pain. The voices of the tormented, and screams from the children, were not something I had expected, nor do I ever wish to experience again. This facility, let alone the staff, isn't equipped to handle half of the patients who were brought here. They have run out of everything, I've been told. They have no pain medicines or bandages." Looking down at the floor in the adjacent room, Sally continued her live coverage,

"There is blood and vomit mixed with feces everywhere you look. Patients are passing away in waiting rooms and in the halls … literally dying without dignity. And the smell is unlike anything I have ever experienced." Forcing back a gag, Sally ended her report by saying, "I'm sorry, I have to get outside for some fresh air. Back to you in New York."

"Thank you, Sally, for that in-depth story. I can't imagine what it's like there.

"Now, we're going to cut over to our sister station in Reno, Nevada with breaking news. Our man on the street is Vince Remmie. I understand you have a person of authority on crisis management with you," Sheldon said as the scene changed to the image of a large metropolitan hospital.

"Ladies and gentlemen, I am standing here with Mr. Gerald Sharkey, the CEO of this major medical center here in Reno. I've been told, Mr. Sharkey, that you are closing your doors here. Why is that?"

"Simple; we have reached overcapacity. We're completely out of supplies. We've tried everything that we know to do, and we just can't get what we need. All of our ventilators are in use, and now we can't get circuits, hoses, tubing, or oxygen." Looking over his shoulder, into the waiting room, Mr. Sharkey continued, his voice taking on a steely edge. "People are dying everywhere in there. We've contacted the Air Force at Langley, but they told us that no supplies are forthcoming."

"Have they given you any idea on when you will see relief?" Vince asked.

"No, they can't give us an ETA on anything. What they have done is advised us that the hospital distribution network has emptied out its warehouses. They said that the demand is insatiable, and growing by the minute. As for this facility, we also don't have the room or the wherewithal to handle any more patients. I'm sorry, I have to get back in there," Mr. Sharkey said shaking his head. He turned on his heel and disappeared inside, closing the door behind him.

Speaking quietly, as if in library, Vince Remmie wrapped up his interview by saying, "There you have it, ladies and gentlemen. Scenes very similar to this are taking place all over the country. Victims of the areas closest to the blast zones, all the way down the line to those affected by fallout, are going to be turned away from the very institutions that are supposed to be there to help them … simply because there are insufficient supplies, beds and medical staff to support a catastrophe such as this."

Sheldon cut in and said, "Vince, thanks for the report. I have our Silver Spring affiliate coming on line, so I'm going to break away from you for the time being. Betty, are you with us?"

"Yes. I'm at the Walter Reed Medical Center, here in Silver Spring. I have just returned from a visit to the Bethesda Navy Medical Center, and I can tell you that both institutions are overflowing with patients, and they just keep coming in, looking for medical help. I have never seen so many people, trying to get medical help, all at the same time.

"Earlier today, I spoke with Civil Response Team Leaders who are absolutely exhausted. They have informed me that all the hospitals in the adjacent areas are turning away casualties. They just don't have the room. The scene, in and around these hospitals, is just shocking," Betty stated with frankness and began a slow walk out of the hospital.

Cutting in to Betty's report, Sheldon said, "Our affiliate in Reno told us the same things are happening there, as well."

"From what I'm witnessing here, it's not surprising, Sheldon. The Army Public Affairs Officer told me that they reached full capacity, here at this site, early yesterday. Today, they are discharging every patient that can travel by Ambulance Bus. It's their effort to get, what they are calling, "regular" patients, out of the areas affected with radiation. They don't need to increase the numbers of the already irradiated population." Standing outside the building, Betty took a deep breath of fresh air and concluded her report. "I don't know how the people that are caring for the sick and injured can tolerate being inside that hospital. The smell is enough to force you out. They must be very special individuals, indeed," Betty said.

Interrupting again, Sheldon said, "Indeed, Betty. We have to cut away for a public service announcement. Don't stay in that danger zone too long."

"Don't worry. I'm heading to the van now. The crew and I will be leaving within the hour," Betty responded.

As he waited for information from the CIA, General Anderson thought about the men and women in the command center of the Pentagon, and how they have, most likely, lost everything dearest to them. The President was lucky. His family had survived the blast, but will they succumb to radiation poisoning? That was an answer he didn't have. He knew they had been evacuated, but was it in time for the antidote to work? The message to the public was issued in as positive a manner as possible to keep some semblance of normalcy in the growing uncertainty. But his conversation with the President had left him stinging and his head reeling.

The President had requested, and was granted, a teleconference with the Healthcare Industry Distributors Association.

Heading up the team was Major Evans, and she provided a very grim report on the state of healthcare and how the U.S. would need to rely upon her allies to get through the aftermath of the attacks.

Knowing he would be making his call shortly after the healthcare update, General Anderson made sure to include a man he knew that could supply answers to some of the hard questions bound to be brought forward, when he made his call.

The President continued his rant. He took up where he left off, raising some interesting questions and making demands which had to be met.

"What in the hell does it mean that we don't have enough supplies to get us through this disaster? Where is the CDC and the supply depots with stockpiles to draw upon in times such as these?" the President demanded, and none too gently.

Before General Anderson could interject, the President continued, speaking loudly into the phone as if raising his voice would supply an answer. "I was told that people with relatively minor doses of radiation, say between seventy to one hundred and twenty rems, have a three in ten chance of experiencing nausea within a few hours of exposure, and as the radiation dosages increase, so do the effects. I have been advised that exposure of three hundred to four hundred rems will cause hair loss, severe diarrhea, ulceration, loss of body fluids and that the probability of death is dramatically increased. But with proper and effective treatment, the survival rate could be one hundred percent. Without these antidotes in place people are going to die by the thousands," the President exclaimed

"Yes sir, I am fully aware of the situation, and we're doing our utmost to get the supplies to the areas that need them the most," General Anderson responded, but was interrupted by a passionate and angry president.

"Why are we trying to scratch together a response, General? I don't understand why there aren't adequate radiological antidotes being pushed forward to the areas in the greatest need. And to top it all off, the lack of equipment and hospital supplies, basic things that should be readily available are completely out of stock. How does something like this happen?"

General Anderson responded candidly, "Mr. President, I'm afraid I'm not smart enough to be able to give you the answers that you are looking for, but I know of someone who is. If you will, sir, he is standing by. I can conference him in."

"That will be most appreciated. I will stand by while you apprise him of the situation," the President said.

The man waiting on hold was none other than Bob Riszko. When General Anderson finished his quick brief on what the President was looking for, Bob knew what he needed to say.

With all the parties now connected, and the introductions made, the President spoke in a more civilized manner, and asked, "Well Mr. Riszko, can you explain to me why we are in such dire straits when it comes to our healthcare supply chain and the support necessary to combat the radiation sickness that many Americans will suffer through?"

"Well Sir, most of the radiological antidotes are in the research and development stage. We have some chelation agents in the national stockpile, but nowhere near enough for an attack of this size. It is my understanding that we have moved all of that material to the National Hospital to try to wash the radiation out of the systems of the Washington, D.C. survivors."

"This is the same treatment that my family is getting, is

that correct?" The President delivered the question more as a statement than a query.

"Yes sir, and I have to warn you, it is very painful therapy," Bob replied. He then added, "We should have done a much better job pre-positioning potassium iodide, and a drug called Prussian Blue, in medical centers in and around all high-risk areas. We didn't even buy enough for one city, let alone two."

The President interrupted, "Explain to me how potassium iodide and Prussian Blue works."

"They block radiation from being absorbed into the thyroid gland and it is thought to lessen the risk of thyroid cancer long term."

The President stopped Bob again. "So millions of Americans, even people outside the hot and warm zones could be looking at a higher risk of cancer later in life?"

"I'm afraid that is the case," Bob replied.

"Holy God. This is going to cause grief and fear for generations," the President said, more to himself than to the men on the other end of the call. He then added, "And what about burn dressings and every other item that we are out of? I'm still trying to understand how something like that can happen."

Bob's response was immediate and forthright. "Mr. President, Sir, it's all because the computers that forecasted our use of supplies were so very accurate. You see, sir, we operated on a "just in time" scenario, so we had 'just enough supplies', of virtually everything, to last a few days of normal treatment. Our supply system operated quite efficiently, even though none of our supply computers could forecast a disaster event of any type. There was nothing extra of anything. We had nowhere near enough to sustain a medical operation of this size. I suspect tight budgets and lack of funds at both the state and federal levels caused the need for just in time solutions."

The President pondered the response and then said, "So our systems are good, so long as there's not an unexpected event? Is that what you're telling me?

Bob replied simply, "That is exactly right, sir."

General Anderson took control of the conversation and added, "As you know, we have sent detailed lists of all the items we need to our allies. They have responded as best they can at such short notice. No one wants to get themselves in the same situation as we are in now, not knowing if they are going to be hit next; therefore, quantities are not what we had hoped for, but supplies and support continue to arrive daily. Our challenge is getting into the areas with the most dire need.

Unable to contain his composure, the President stormed, "Damn it! How does a country like America get caught without supplies and equipment, when DHS knew for years this was likely to happen? And now, tens of thousands of Americans will pay for this dereliction of duty with their lives. Millions will worry for the rest of their lives about cancer for themselves and birth defects for their children." Thinking of his own children, the President lost his composure and wept while the General made no attempt at bravado.

A call from Langley was scheduled to take place soon. General Anderson had been told that at an analyst, Tim Rausch, had uncovered information worth reporting to the President. He knew that finding the perpetrator behind this attack was just the tip of the iceberg. Not only was there a military response looming large upon the horizon, but the issue of hundreds of thousands of citizens, sick and dying, was also imminent. Would there be enough doctors, nurses, medical supplies and pain medication to treat the population that needed it the most? People closest to the blast sites will certainly feel inclined to head to the clinics at the first sign of anything abnormal, putting an enormous burden on an already overloaded situation. And as the demand for food and supplies grew, he wondered if there would there would be rioting in the streets as brother turned against brother trying to be the one to get that last can of baby formula or jar of peanut butter to feed the kids even if it meant taking it, by force, from your neighbor.

He also wondered how the rest of the world would respond. He knew that, historically, the United States was very generous and always ready to help others when the call came for aid, be it food, supplies or monetary. And, typically, America handled internal crises within her own borders; but this time, things would be different and he hoped that no offer of assistance would be turned away.

From the level of destruction he had witnessed earlier, General Anderson knew that they were going to need every able-bodied individual and all supplies offered. Experts on various issues ranging from social to medical would be needed. So far, the President had accepted all offers, but the crisis was still young and he knew it would last for some time with the need growing in the days and weeks to come. How long would our allies be able to continue to send supplies without causing a strain on their own stores?

As he awaited the call from CIA Headquarters his mind churned over the hundreds of questions of which there were only speculative answers.

. . .

As the clocked ticked its way into another post-attack sunrise, it had become quite obvious that the numbers of sick and dying was growing faster than could be dealt with. Offers to provide assistance continued pouring in from Canada, Australia, Germany, the United Kingdom, Japan and other countries. The President accepted any and all aid, but the logistics of getting it into the country, and then out to the areas that needed it the most would take time, and that was something the people in the hardest hit areas didn't have. Knowing that the country was in desperate need of information about how he was handling the disaster, the President insisted upon sending a message to the public. He asked General Anderson to schedule another news conference to detail the situation.

Gathering in the media center at NORTHCOM, General Anderson greeted the press once again. "Good morning ladies and gentlemen. Let me begin by thanking you all for taking the time to come here. First and foremost, the President has asked that I send his deepest condolences to those families out there that have lost relatives and friends in this horrendous attack. Rest assured, the President is safe and running the country from the confines of NORAD in Colorado. The First Family is also safe and in a secure location, under medical observation; just to ensure that they will not suffer any long term affects from radiation. So far, I am told, the prognosis is very good. They ought to be able to rejoin the President in a couple of days.

"Now, let's get down to the business at hand. The situation in Washington and Las Vegas is growing extremely grim. As you know, there are tens of thousands of victims, and that number is growing daily. Our ability to evacuate more than a few hundred per day, to hospitals outside of the affected areas, is limited. The reason is due to the levels of radiological elements in both attack zones. It is too high for standard evacuation procedures by EMS teams. We had to call in specially trained Civil Support and other specialized response teams from the DoD and National Guard units in the surrounding states. However, due to the nature of the afflicted, triage, classification, and transportation has proved to be difficult."

A hand went up in the sea of reporters, so General Anderson took a question from Cynthia, a print media journalist. "Sir, I have seen people in auditoriums, churches and school gymnasiums, all over the D.C. area. They are without doctors or even nurses to care for them. And what's worse, there are no pain relievers for these people. The scenes that I have personally witnessed are gruesome and the level of suffering is beyond belief. What is being done to get help to these people?"

General Anderson looked Cynthia in the eye when he gave his response. "I'm afraid that there is a very limited supply of the highly effective pain remedies, like Morphine. I've been informed that hospitals have also run out of virtually all medical supplies, not just drugs and medications, but the basics, things like bandages. The distribution network is trying to bring in stock from other areas of the country, but the demand is immeasurable. It's higher than we could ever have anticipated. At the rate the medical supplies are being used, the entire healthcare supply chain will be completely dried up."

Tony, the roving reporter, raised his hand, eager to ask a question. "General, sir, why don't you just open up the DoD supply depots? Wouldn't that make sense at a time like this?"

"Yes, it would, were there a supply depot to tap into. For

lack of a better explanation, they were, in effect, closed back in 1992. The military hospitals have been using commercial healthcare suppliers and distributors since then, just like any other healthcare organization in the U.S. I can tell you that we have requested support from the CDC's strategic national stockpile, but they have very little in the way of opiates such as Oxycontin, Demerol, Percocet or Morphine, which I had mentioned earlier."

"General," a shout came from the back of the room. "Are you telling us that you are simply going to let these people suffer and die in pain?"

"That's not what I said at all, young man. The President has received offers from other nations to aid in relief and he has accepted every offer that as been put forth. But, it isn't an easy task. There are protocols that must be adhered to and followed. As much as we would like to, we simply cannot bring in these high-level drugs and just start handing them out. Once received and verified, they must be moved into the locations that need them the most. You must believe that we are doing our utmost to get the help into the areas that have the greatest need. In addition, many of our allies have sent volunteers, doctors and others who have offered to help get the sick into safe zones. These fine folks need to be briefed and have their protective gear checked out before being deployed into the field. All of this takes time and effort."

Master Sergeant Wolfe, a staff member, approached General Anderson and whispered something in his ear. With a nod, General Anderson then turned to the group assembled before him and said, "I'm sorry to have to cut this short. Thank you for coming." He turned and left the room buzzing with unanswered questions.

As the two men walked down the hall, General Anderson said, "Whom did you say the President just spoke with?"

"General Adam Spencer, sir. Apparently, he's been appointed as Medical Commander at the National Hospital, and has been put in charge of overseeing all aspects of the medical side of this disaster for both D.C. and Las Vegas. The President wanted you to speak with General Spencer about the lack of response. The President feels that you are his eyes and ears out here."

"Me, huh?" General Anderson grunted.

"Yes sir. You seem to have answered all of the President's questions. You certainly know a lot about what's going on out there, at all levels."

"I make it my business to know," General Anderson responded gruffly.

The two men rounded the corner and entered a secured office. Setting the phone on speaker, Master Sergeant Wolfe dialed the number to General Spencer's office. After the first ring, General Spencer answered the call.

Responding, General Anderson said, "Hello Adam, this is Ted Anderson."

Getting right to the point, General Spencer said, "Good to hear from you, Ted. The President tells me that you've been to ground zero in D.C. What can you tell me about the situation out there?"

"I'd say 'about what you'd expect,' but to be honest, it was far worse than anything you could imagine. The blast took out the entire Mall area, and everything within approximately a two mile radius, was completely annihilated. The people who were not killed immediately by the blast, I'd say that by now, they're dead."

General Spencer agreed.

Continuing, General Anderson said, "The rescue teams are trying to make their way into the city, but they have many obstacles to get around. Since the attack, we have experienced great difficulty evacuating casualties due to very extensive grid-lock in the National Capitol Region. The high radiation levels have prevented us from getting wreckers onto the beltway. Therefore, evacuation of the most seriously wounded govern-ment workers has to be accomplished entirely by helicopter. Rescue of the citizenry has been impossible. As a result, most of the population of D.C. has endured prolonged exposure to dangerously high levels of ionizing radiation. Health science experts, in the field of acute radiation sickness, have advised the President that the death toll in D.C., and the immediate surrounding areas, will exceed one million."

"I understand, Ted. Thanks to you, and your team's quick response, the Special Radiological Response Units from the Marine Corps were able to rescue the First Family as well as some of the White House Staff. We believe that, due to special safe rooms in the White House, most, but not all, of those folks will survive.

"The First Family, the surviving White House staff and approximately 25 Congresspersons are here receiving treat-ment. I'm told that the Congress and the Supreme Court were in session, and that ground zero had been selected to facili-tate devastation of all federal buildings. We have a handful of survivors in Congress who were in the basement area of their office buildings. They are all in very critical condition and are receiving the most intensive care possible. As I said, not all are going to survive.

"Further, the attack on Las Vegas was quite destructive in

its own right. There were very high casualty rates in hotels, as designed by the terrorists who perpetrated this horrific act. The combination of air blast and the associated blast injuries were devastating to both guests and staff on the Los Vegas Strip. Guests in the hotels, away from the strip, had a much higher initial survivor rate. But the extremely high radiation levels were less contained than was the case in Washington. Therefore, the immediate absorption of radiation created enormous fatalities in the first day. The hospitals in Las Vegas were either destroyed or inundated with walking wounded within the first hours after the attack. Hospitals between Las Vegas and Reno were also quickly overwhelmed. As the media has been reporting, many major medical centers have closed their doors, not allowing for new patients because they are overcapacity, under staffed and out of supplies.

"Civil Support Teams from the Nevada, Arizona, New Mexico and California National Guard units performed admirably, but post-attack survivor rates in Las Vegas were unfortunately very high."

Hoping that things were getting better in the field, General Anderson asked, "Can you give me a précis on the supply situation as you see it?"

"Well, Ted, we're still experiencing systemic shortages of medical supplies and the equipment needed to effectively treat acute radiological sickness. As you may be aware, our healthcare supply system is not designed to sustain extremely high spikes in demand, or the very high usage rates of the magnitude we are experiencing today. It is apparent that manufacturing of medical supplies and equipment cannot surge for 6 to 9 months to meet the demand let alone replenish all of our distributors' stock.

"There are no stocks of Morphine or other drugs to alleviate pain. Our care providers are triaging the patients who will likely suffer longest. The suffering is intolerable and the effect on healthcare providers' morale is profound. That's an additional burden which I have to find a way to deal with. If you have any ideas, Ted, I'm open to suggestions."

General Anderson said, "Trust me, Adam, we've been struggling through that very same scenario as we try to get the supplies from our allies brought in and then sent back out to the areas in the most dire need. Yours is a difficult position to be in, I'm sure."

"The obstacles are not insurmountable, but there are challenges. For instance, there are no ventilators which are not spoken for. Hospitals in outlying areas are being told by their suppliers that there just aren't any stores left in the National Capitol Region, and that all distributors are depleted. Patients and staff in D.C. area hospitals are deceased or in the process of dying. We need Morphine and any other opiate pain relievers we can get our hands on. We're totally out. I'm sure you've heard that patients are dying, by huge numbers, in agony. And the staff in all areas of hospital care is stressed to the maximum. There are hundreds of staff members totally burned out. Patient care is almost nonexistent and we've only just seen the tip of the iceberg.

"I'm sure you are well aware that we are out of stock in following products, and in order to continue with any level of intervention, we need: IV fluids, Sodium Chloride, ringers, sterile water, burn and wound dressings, regular bandages—any type can be made to work. We desperately need ventilators, vent circuits and endotracheal tubes of all sizes; oxygen cylinders and tubing, burn creams and antibiotics. We will need to recruit thousands of bone marrow donors for the patients who will likely survive if we can transplant bone marrow and reestablish their immune systems.

"As you know, we have solicited aid to help us with comfort care items such as pain medications. We also asked for additional supplies, the things needed to treat burns and other wounds which are in increasingly high demand. However, survival rates of the general population in heavily populated areas of Washington D.C., and throughout neighborhoods in Las Vegas, adjacent to the Strip, will unfortunately, be very low."

General Anderson listened intently and after taking it all in said, "I understand your frustration. I have heard it from other doctors heading up care facilities all over the country. Our allies are responding to our call for aid, but as I stated earlier, it takes time to get things where they're needed the most. We have teams at staging depots and they are working around the clock to get supplies into the field. "

General Spencer asked, "Can you give me an idea of what you see from your side? How are you managing this?"

"We have teams from national distributors which have deployed to Philadelphia and Phoenix They are there to run receipts and input the donated supplies and equipment for further distribution. They have set up a mobile distribution center and are in the early stages of receiving orders from hospitals that are treating casualties from D.C. and Las Vegas. The system is functioning, but this is an ad hoc system and will take a few days before the materials arrive at the requesting hospitals. The toughest job for these folks is trying to provide materials to alternate care centers that have sprung up in churches, auditoriums and community centers. These places were not in any distributors' supply network before this catastrophe; consequently, no one knows about them. The bottom line is that by the time a supply chain is reestablished, it will be too late for everyone except the folks that would have survived without treatment. I am sad to say, the death toll will be of galactic proportions."

After a brief pause, to take double check his notes, General Spencer added, "The President asked me specifically, what steps are being taken to help the physically and mentally handicapped? Can you brief me on that?"

"We've had questions come in from Disability Rights groups regarding how we are helping this specific population. Quite frankly, Adam, we don't have much to offer at this juncture. Reports of relatives trying frantically to get into the affected areas to rescue family members have been thwarted. We have anecdotal information that most of those with disabilities remained in their homes. The ensuing chaos was terrible and nobody knew where the handicapped people lived. Some were rescued by neighbors and friends, but almost everyone is dying in the intercity area, except for those who were lucky enough to be in areas searched by the Civil Support Teams. Unfortunately, many will die anyway due to their proximity to the blast zone and doses of radiation they received."

"Do you have the numbers on the death toll for that population?" General Spencer asked.

"We only have estimates at this time and that number is in the tens of thousands," General Anderson answered solemnly.

General Spencer exhaled, "My God; that many of our most vulnerable citizens died in their homes?"

"That's the number we believe to be correct. Almost everyone that remained in the city is dead or dying or will die in days, maybe weeks, depending where they were when the detonation occurred. They have been absorbing radiation for several days now with no protection. It's a situation that defies understanding."

General Spencer said, "I wish we could get pain killers in here quicker. The screams of the dying are unbearable and it's traumatizing our staff. We have volunteers who are arriving, not just from this country, but from all over the world. Those who joined the rescue units can only stay for a couple days and then we have to take them off the line. It's brutal duty." Being extremely frank, General Spencer continued, "Ted, I've had reports that, in some locations, there are people asking to be put out of their misery. They know they are dying, they are in terrible pain and there isn't anything the medical providers can do to help. It's frustrating to my team and, quite frankly, they feel as though there isn't enough being done at your level to help them get the supplies they desperately need."

"I've heard about that as well, Adam, and believe me, we are moving as fast as we can. We are hindered by a number of issues which we are attacking one by one. We are pushing forward into the depots as quickly as we can.

"By the way, have you heard of a group of folks that have come together calling themselves the Angels of Mercy?" General Anderson asked.

"No, I haven't. But to be honest, I'm more concerned with my team getting care to the masses. Unfortunately, I haven't had time to keep up with the news lately," General Spencer said.

"That may be a blessing, but what I have to say is indirectly related to your comment. This group wanders through churches, the school gyms and civic centers where makeshift hospitals have been established. It's there that they look for their victims, and offer to end the suffering. They then carry the afflicted outside, away from the rest of the sick and dying, and end it for them, usually with a gunshot to the head." General Anderson had to stop for a moment to collect his thoughts and composure before continuing. Rubbing his brow, he said, "They then load the bodies onto a flatbed truck and transport them to one of the mass grave sites that have been popping up all over the outskirts of the city, to be incinerated, along with the rest of the nameless. The number of dead is increasing, exponentially, every day. It's the only way they know of to dispose of all the bodies."

General Spencer said, "What has FEMA been doing to help?"

"Between the military and FEMA, they are trying to curb the instances of mass graves being created by the locals. We have just started the process of trying to bury the dead in some organized, civilized manner, and not just dumped into a hole in the ground to be cremated. FEMA has activated special mortuary affairs teams from across America, but identifying remains and instituting a grave registry is going to take some time, most likely months, so it will be a task to keep the local citizenry from continuing on their current path of burying their dead in unmarked, mass graves," General Anderson replied.

General Spencer interrupted to add a side note. He could sense the stress in General Anderson's voice. "Ted, just so you know, we are ramping up our mental health services in anticipation of widespread Post Traumatic Stress Disorder. It will be available for all staff in all areas of consequence management, specifically the healthcare sector, but it is certainly there for anyone exhibiting PTSD. They will have access to any and all help. That goes for you, too, Ted. Don't think you're out there alone. In this line of work, we could all use a helping hand from time-to-time, and this is the least we can do to offer aid to those closest to the disaster."

With a half-smile, General Anderson said, "Thanks Adam. I'll keep that in mind."

"One last thing," General Spencer remarked. "The amount of infectious waste has become an issue. To be honest, it's overwhelming, and it is causing an enormous public health emergency. It's affecting not only the hospitals and care centers, but entire neighborhoods as well. We need far more full protective suits than what is currently on hand."

Nodding his head, General Anderson said, "Yes, I have been briefed on that as well. I can assure you, we have added the suits to the list of things we have asked for from our allies.

"The need for an increase in the number of mortuary teams has not gone unnoticed, but as you said, we just don't have the materials to supply them right now The EPA has also stepped up. They are sending environmental engineers into affected areas immediately to develop a hazardous waste disposal plan. Hopefully this plan, and our DoD transportation assets, will restore sanitation to these areas and avert a Public Health disaster within this disaster. But, for now, I have to get back to conference center. . The President promised a radio broadcast. He wants to keep the country informed and I want to hear what he has to say."

"Okay, Ted, but remember what I said about PTSD. I'll be in touch," General Spencer said and hung up the phone.

Later that day, as promised, the President made the radio broadcast letting America, and the world, know he was still alive and in charge. He began his speech simply. "My fellow Americans, I come before you tonight, not only as your President, but also as a fellow citizen. I have no speech writers or aides to prompt me, so please, bear with me.

"Like many of you, my life and that of my family, has been dramatically affected by this terrible act against our country. My family is currently undergoing treatment for severe radiation exposure, along with several of my personal staff, and I cannot tell you with any level of confidence that they will survive. We have hope that things will turn out for the best for each of them. Certainly, there will be the mental and emotional scars, but the physical impact will not be known for some time to come. Your prayers are appreciated. For those of you who have lost family members, either in Washington or in Nevada, I wish them Godspeed.

"For those of you in the hospital now, or those who will need medical care in the coming days, weeks or months, I can assure you, your government, although crippled at the moment, is doing everything it possibly can to get the necessary supplies into the areas that are in gravest need. In the meantime, there are teams of men and women, working round the clock, going into the hot zones, looking for survivors. Those people are being transported, via any means necessary, to available hospitals within the continental United States. I'm saddened to say that most of the people being rescued will not survive. We will do our best to get them the care they need so that they can die with dignity and without suffering. But it is a daunting task, so please be patient.

"I also want to mention that the roads are slowly being cleared of vehicles that were rendered useless due to the electromagnetic pulse caused by the nuclear blasts. I ask that you respect the workers and let them do their job. And, please, stay away from Las Vegas and Washington D.C. proper. I know that many of you had homes and family in those areas, and although it feels like an eternity has passed, it has only been ten days. It is still extremely dangerous out there and without the proper protective gear, you are taking a risk that could ultimately claim your life. If you believe someone from your immediate family could still be in a hot zone, the Red Cross and other agencies are opening help lines that you can call for information on the people who have been rescued to date as well as provide data on those who live in the area that you have not heard from. A list of phone numbers will be provided after this broadcast, so stay tuned for that.

"I fully realize that there will be shortages of things that we, as a nation, have taken for granted. Right now, our hospitals are without many of the items that they need to care for the number of afflicted. Our first and foremost concern is getting the supplies, sent by our friends and allies from around the world, into the areas that need them the most. If you are capable of volunteering your time or expertise, check with the Red Cross to see if they can use your help. There are many things that you, as an individual, can do. Giving blood is a great start." After a momentary pause, to give the audience a chance to take in what he had said, the President added, "In conclusion my fellow Americans, please help each other as best you can, neighbor to neighbor, brother to brother, friend to friend."

The airwaves were turned over to the local radio stations which began the process of providing phone numbers of the support agencies in each area.

Immediately following the radio broadcast of the President's speech, Tim, Jessie and Stan were making their final preparations for their briefing with the President. Seated at a table, in a secured conference room at CIA Headquarters, they awaited the President who was going to join them via teleconference.

Tim opened his briefcase, removed several journals and placed them on the conference table in front of him. Each of the journals had colored tabs marking specific pages with information he felt would be of value. The pages were dated providing a timeline of events as Tim saw them unfolding.

Pointing to the stack of notebooks on the table, Stan asked, "What the hell is all that?"

Tim answered bluntly, "My notes."

"Notes," Stan replied in a typical, humorless, retort.

"Yeah, notes. Everything is right here," Tim said, patting the cover of the topmost book.

"You know, I could have your job for pulling a stunt like this," Stan said.

"Yeah, but you won't," Tim replied with a sardonic grin.

Jessie just shook her head and didn't offer any commentary of her own. She knew when to keep out of a conversation, and this was one of those times. She knew Tim had gotten into the habit of taking notes in college, and he was quite good at it, so she wasn't surprised to learn that he hadn't changed. He would make a terrible field agent, she thought. He's too predictable.

Just before the appointed time, Andrew Winton entered the room. Taking a seat in front of the console, he had every intention of being in control of the telecon.

Right on schedule, the large video screen came alive and the face of the President was before them. His appearance was that of man who had aged many years in just the few days since the attacks on the United States. His face was pale and drawn, his eyes showing the strain from lack of sleep, but he was alert and ready for the call.

The President opened the meeting by saying, "Hello Andrew. I see you have your team assembled. Please, introduce us."

"Yes, sir," Andrew said and pointed to each person as he went around the room, making their introductions. He purposefully left Tim for last.

"Ah, Mr. Rausch," the President said. "I've heard a lot about you these last few days. They tell me you have compelling evidence regarding Hezbollah, the perpetrators of this attack against our sovereignty. Please, start at the beginning and don't leave anything out. I'm interested in hearing anything you think may be of importance, no matter how minor or insignificant it may appear. And, take your time."

Thinking he would be nervous, Tim found that he was completely calm. He began his dissertation with the boxing match in Germany and how he had found the combination of Abu al Mussari and Anatoly Buskeyev to be of concern. It was from that point forward that he watched and learned. Tim went though his journals, line item by line item while the President listened with the utmost attention, only interrupting to make sure he had not misunderstood a statement or an event, all the while jotting notes of his own.

More than an hour had elapsed when Tim finally wrapped up the call by playing the conversation between the Karpenkos and Abu al Mussari at the luxury condo in Dubai.

The President directed his next question to Andrew, saying, "So, you had these guys all along. Why were we not watching them a little more closely? Surely Mr. Rausch came to you with his concerns?"

Andrew responded quickly, "Mr. President, your predecessor made it clear that we were to focus our attention on al Qaeda. That, sir, is precisely what we did."

Turning his attention back to Tim, the President asked, "I don't see anything in your presentation about how the bombs came to be in the U.S. We know they came from Russia, but how did they get into the country?"

Tim hesitated, so Stan intervened. "It is our estimation that they arrived either by one of our ports or through Mexico. Due to the timing of the scenario, as Tim had pointed out, the weapons could have been here well before 9-11, when we weren't monitoring our ports and borders as closely as we are now. They then secreted the weapons away to some hiding place until Hezbollah was ready to use them. One thing that we do know about these terror groups, Sir, is that they are very patient."

"Understood,' the President said while making another note. He then asked, "Do we know who detonated the bombs, or how they got them into place without being seen?"

Again, Stan responded, "No Sir, and that part of the puzzle will be more difficult to piece together since everything for miles around the blast zone had been destroyed. We have no video cameras or eyewitnesses to fall back on. As you know, terror cells within the U.S. have been steadily on the rise. With the help of our sister agency, the FBI, I'm confident we will uncover the triggermen." Stan detected a look of scorn when he glanced over at Tim.

"I see. Well, I believe I have the information I need to be able to make a sound decision regarding how to proceed. Our response will be swift and final." Then, looking directly at Tim, the President said, "Thank you for your undaunted efforts in finding the ones responsible, Mr. Rausch. The Nation owes you a debt of gratitude."

"Well, sir, I did have help. I couldn't have done it without the field personnel in Dubai," Tim said, giving Jessie some of the recognition.

"Ah, yes. And thank you, as well, Ms. Coltrane," the President said with a slight smile and then bade them a good day.

As they walked down the corridor, Stan said, "Looks like you got your name in the history books, you two. Good job."

Rancor sharpened Tim's voice. "Bullshit, Stan. What the hell good is that? My name goes down in history as the agent who could have averted the worst attack against his country but fell short."

Jessie took Tim by the arm and kept him moving. "It's not your fault, Tim. No one would listen to you."

They walked the brightly lit, sterile-looking corridors until they were back in Tim's office. Suddenly, he was overcome with an irresistible desire to kiss her, and he sensed that she was feeling the same. He could feel it in her presence. The hell with it, he thought, and took her into his arms and pressed his lips to hers in a passionate kiss. Jessie didn't put up a fight. She returned his ardent kiss, running her hands through his hair, but then abruptly pulled away. She turned to face the wall, her arms folded squarely against her breasts.

"What are you doing?" Jessie asked flatly.

Her words didn't register on his dizzied senses. "What do you mean? I just kissed you," Tim responded plainly, as if his actions required explanation.

"Exactly! I get the distinct impression it was a lot more than 'thanks for a job well done,'" Jessie remarked, sarcastically.

Tim fumbled for the words. "Jess, I …"

Standing behind Tim's desk, Jessie took control of the conversation. "I know what's going through your mind because the same thoughts have been going through mine. But Tim, you know as well as I do that this will never work … on so many levels, it can never work."

Tim let out an audible sigh.

"Believe me, I wanted you, too. But that was a long time ago and so many things have changed since our days in college."

Tim wanted to respond, but still couldn't find the words, so he just let Jessie do the talking. She always was quite good at it.

"For one thing, you're married; and for another, you have two great kids."

"We're separated," Tim interjected halfheartedly, not really knowing why he mentioned it.

"Oh, excuse me? I have known married couples that weren't as together as you and Donna, even considering the separation. Come on, Tim. You can't fool me, but more importantly, you can't fool yourself. We're not kids anymore, and this isn't college. Times have changed. Your family will need you now, more than ever. I'm not going to be the one to come between you and them. To do anything different would destroy you and I can't let that happen."

"I love you, Jess. I always have, but you're right, you know. I am committed to my family and I do love them," Tim said.

Softening her tone and relaxing into an easy smile, Jessie said, "I'll let you love me, Tim, but it can only be as a friend. Let's keep it at that, shall we?" but inside her heart was aching.

She knew she was letting go, for the last time, the only man she ever really cared about. The only man she truly loved.

"I believe I can do that," Tim said, returning the smile.

• • •

After a long, grueling day at work, Donna sat in front of the television with her children and sister, Eva, watching the latest news reports. She surfed around the various channels, viewing reports on network TV and the cable news outlets. She, like most of America, spent every free moment glued to the tube. She cared about how the people, closest to the bombings, were faring and if there was any new information regarding the perpetrator of this heinous action. Since it had been close to a month since the bombing, she was interested in learning what America's response to this attack would be. Speculation and rumor ran rampant, but tonight, the President was going to address the nation with a State of the Union speech. It would be the first time the President's face will have been seen on television since the bombings took place just four weeks earlier, but it seemed a lifetime ago. Until that appointed hour, Donna couldn't settle on any one station for long as she surfed the channels looking for the perfect telecast.

Finally, the news conference began. The President was sitting behind a desk, facing the camera, ready to speak.

"Oh good," Donna said, letting out an exasperated sigh.

"What's the matter?" Eva questioned.

"I thought we missed the beginning of the President's speech," Donna said, turning up the volume.

"Well, if you'd quit surfing around the channels, you wouldn't miss anything," Eva added teasingly.

"Yeah, Mom learned from the best," Scott interjected with an approving laugh.

"Shhhh," Donna said as the trio laughed. Knowing it was at her expense, she started to laugh, too.

When the laughter settled, they turned their attention back to the television. There were no reporters present, no fanfare or any of the other familiar faces usually present at an event such as this. The only things in the room were the American Flag and the Great Seal of the United States displayed prominently behind the desk where the President would be seated.

After a few moments of silence, the President entered the room as the cameras rolled. Placing his notes in front of him on the desk, the President began his speech. "Good evening my fellow Americans. Tonight, I come to you with news I am certain you have been anxiously awaiting. I'm sure you're wondering if we know who is behind these heinous acts. After an in-depth conversation with the CIA, I am convinced, beyond any reasonable doubt, that we were attacked by Hezbollah. Our intelligence has proven that they have had terror cells, embedded here within our borders, for quite some time. This is the same group known as the Iranian Supreme Cultural Revolution Council which had taken responsibility for the attack against Israel in the hours prior to the bombings here in America.

"Knowing this, I have placed our Armed Forces on DEFCON 1, a war footing which will require a wartime response. Similarly, I have placed calls to the Ambassadors of Russia, China, Israel and South Korea to let them know I will not, nor will the people of the country, tolerate such an act of terror against our nation. As I speak to you, my fellow Americans, B-2 Bombers, outfitted with nuclear weapons, are dropping their payloads upon Tehran, Iran. In addition, bombers carrying incendiary and high explosive bombs have taken out the nuclear facilities in Syria and North Korea. I have received word from our commanding generals that the objective has been achieved in that regard.

"You are probably wondering if there has been collateral damage due to these strikes. Unfortunately, the answer to that question is yes. Innocent lives are usually lost when leaders choose to go down such a road.

"The world has once again witnessed the will and the might of the United States. We may be down, but we are not out. Never will we be out!

"In the meantime, here at home, we will rebuild. We have learned some hard and terrible lessons. Our number one priority right now is to get our medical systems back on line. As most of the country has learned, we are experiencing severe shortages of everything from basic wound care to intensive pain medications.

"Our allies from around the world have come forth and offered aid. Not only have they sent supplies, but support personnel as well, to help a medical system that was on the verge of collapse. But, with time, we will heal, and we will all look back on that day and see how far forward we have come."

The President continued to speak and as Donna listened she knew it was her Tim who had provided the data; her Tim that had been the one to nail the bad guys. She was bursting with pride for her husband and his determination. She had finally come to grips with his personality and accepted him for the man he was. She placed a call to Tim's office to tell him, personally.

• • •

After a few days of debriefings, Tim was finally able to escort Jessie to the plane for her return trip to Dubai. As they waited for the call to board, they stood side-by-side in silence, each thinking their own thoughts. When the call came, Jessie knew this would be the last time she would ever see Tim.

"It was great to see you again," Jessie said. "I hate that it had to be under such dire circumstances, though."

"I agree," Tim responded, but he didn't know what else to say. Many things that he wanted to say ran through his mind, but he knew it was best to leave them be.

Jessie asked, teasingly, "So, do you think you can give me a hug or should I just expect a handshake goodbye? I don't want to be the cause of any embarrassment, especially here in public."

That statement alone caused the color to rise under Tim's collar. To avoid further humiliation at Jessie's hand, Tim gave her a hug and sent her on her way.

He watched as the plane taxied down the runway and then took to the air. "Bye Jess," he said and then walked to his car to drive home to his empty apartment.

Spring 2011

Rain soaked leaves glistened in the emerging light as the sun broke through the thick, gray, clouds. Tim sat on the balcony of his new apartment awaiting the arrival of his family. He had just been on the phone with Donna. She said hey were on the road, and less than an hour away. In the year following the attack, either he would drive up to Wisconsin to visit the family or Donna would drive down to Langley to spend a long weekend with him; and sometimes she would surprise him and arrive without the kids. Tim finally had enough of the road trips and wanted to know if they were ready to come home. When asked about the fallout north of Langley, where he now lived, Tim advised that it was not at a level to be concerned with, so Donna agreed.

After the attack, things got out of hand in most places around the country. Everyday items became scarce and people panicked. At one point, the President had to declare a national state of emergency and imposed a mandatory curfew in the areas closest to the bombings. Military police patrolled the streets both day and night, and anyone caught breaking the curfew was arrested, no questions asked. But even with the military patrols, there were still sporadic incidents of rioting. As with every disaster, this one included, people looted and plundered the vacant homes and businesses with complete disregard for their own safety which resulted in the need for the National Guard to come in and settle things down.

It took time, and with the help from America's allies which continued to provide basic goods, things slowly began to return to normal. Trucks carrying food and clothing could travel without an armed escort. Grocery stores and retail outlets were once again opening and selling their wares at reasonable rates and the black market was drying up.

Tim walked into the living room and turned on the television. It was time for the evening news. As the commercials droned on, he went to the kitchen for a cold drink and when he returned, what he saw on the screen turned his blood cold.

Today was the day the President was going to unveil his choice for the site of the new White House and home of the federal government. Reporters were on the scene at the place where the Declaration of Independence was signed and they were poised to ask questions. The camera cut away from the reporters and panned the scene outside. Standing there, in amongst the crowd of spectators at Independence Hall in Philadelphia, was a face Tim recognized ... a face he would never forget.

It was the face of Abu al Mussari.